*"Office romances a
never—"*

"Stop." Tom put his index finger against her lips.

"But I—"

"Shh. Listen. Are you listening?"

Shelly made a face at him. "Hit me with it."

"I have examples."

"Of?"

"Office romances that worked out great. Better than great. Let's see…Jack Hanson and his wife, Samantha. Samantha and Jack were old business rivals. Then she came to work at Hanson Media— with Jack. And then there's David Hanson, George Hanson's brother. He actually married his secretary, Nina. Can you believe that?"

"Okay, okay. I'll modify my position."

"You bet you will."

"*Sometimes* office romances do work out. How's that?"

"Better."

She cleared her throat. "So. Are you going to…kiss me again?"

Dear Reader,

Some of you may have enjoyed the FAMILY BUSINESS miniseries that came out a couple of years ago. I certainly did.

Now, FAMILY BUSINESS is going BACK TO BUSINESS, an all-new six-book series beginning this month. Silhouette offers you six passionate, heartwarming love stories from some of your favorite Special Edition authors.

In this first installment, *In Bed with the Boss,* smart, pretty single mom Shelly Winston gets an inside tip on the job of her dreams and goes to work for hunky CFO Tom Holloway. But trouble in the person of Tom's longtime nemesis could derail all their hopes and destroy any future they might someday share.

Only love and trust—and truth—can save the day.

Yours always,

Christine Rimmer

USA TODAY BESTSELLING AUTHOR

CHRISTINE RIMMER

IN BED WITH THE BOSS

SPECIAL EDITION

Published by Silhouette Books

America's Publisher of Contemporary Romance

Special thanks and acknowledgment
to Christine Rimmer for her contribution
to the BACK IN BUSINESS miniseries.

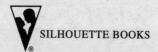 SILHOUETTE BOOKS

ISBN-13: 978-0-373-24909-1
ISBN-10: 0-373-24909-8

IN BED WITH THE BOSS

CHRISTINE RIMMER

came to her profession the long way around. Before settling down to write about the magic of romance, she'd been everything, including an actress, a salesclerk and a waitress. Now that she's finally found work that suits her perfectly, she insists she never had a problem keeping a job—she was merely gaining "life experience" for her future as a novelist. Christine is grateful not only for the joy she finds in writing, but for what waits when the day's work is through: a man she loves, who loves her right back, and the privilege of watching their children grow and change day to day. She lives with her family in Oklahoma. Visit Christine at www.christinerimmer.com.

For Tom and Ed,
who never fail to comfort
and inspire.

Prologue

Two years ago...

It was *the* moment.

And Tom Holloway knew it.

Across the black granite boardroom table, Helen Taka-Hanson waited, her beautiful face composed, showing him nothing. Behind her, beyond the floor-to-ceiling windows, the afternoon sun reflected off the tall buildings of North Michigan Avenue. Tom kept his gaze level, on Helen. But he knew what was out there: The Second City. The Magnificent Mile.

Chicago. Tom wanted it. *Needed* it, really. A fresh start in a new town. He would be chief financial officer of TAKA-Hanson's new hospitality division.

Which meant hotels. Contemporary luxury hotels on a grand scale. It was the biggest venture he'd tackled so far and it sounded good. Better than good.

And the job was his. Helen had already made the offer.

What he said next could blow it for him—more than likely *would* blow it for him. Which was why he'd left the crucial information off his résumé. His disgrace had happened so long ago, it was easily glossed over now.

But Tom had learned the hard way that concealment didn't work in the long term. The high-stakes world of finance was too damn small. In the end, his past always found him.

Better to show his stuff first, let them know he had the chops, get all the way to the job offer. And then take a deep breath and lay the bad news right out there.

The offer just might stand in spite of his past. If it didn't, if he lost the job, well, chances were he would have lost it anyway in the end, when the ugly facts surfaced.

Oh, yeah. A delicate moment, this. The moment of truth.

Helen said, "Well, Tom. You've heard our offer. Is there anything else we need to go over?"

Tom sat back in the chair, ordered his body to relax and told himself—for the hundredth time—that it had to be done.

"As a matter of fact, Helen. There is something else…"

She arched a brow at him and waited for him to go on.

He said, "I was fired once. It was a long time ago, my first job out of Princeton."

"Fired." Helen spoke the word flatly. "That's not on your résumé, is it?"

"No. And it gets worse."

"I'm listening."

"I was young and way too hungry, working on Wall Street, determined to make it big and do it fast. None of which is any justification for my actions. I was discharged for insider trading. And then I was arrested for it. And convicted. I did six months."

A silence. A pretty long one. Tom could feel yet another great job slipping away from him.

At last, Helen asked the big question. "Were you guilty?"

"Yes. I was."

He might have softened the harsh fact a little. He could have explained what a naive idiot he'd been then. He could have told her all about his mentor at the time, who'd convinced him to pass certain "tips" to big clients. He could have said that the guy got away clean by setting Tom up to take the fall for him. That the same former mentor had been a curse on his life since then. Because of that one man, Tom had lost out on a number of opportunities—and not just in terms of his career. It would have been the truth.

However, his former boss wasn't the one up for CFO, TAKA-Hanson, hospitality division. Tom was. His prospective employer needed to know that he'd once broken the law—and then gone to jail for it. The why and the wherefore?

Not the question.

Tom sat unflinching, waiting for the ax to fall.

Instead, Helen smiled.

It was a slow smile, and absolutely genuine—a warm smile, the kind of smile that would make any red-blooded man sit up and take notice. From what Tom had heard, this genius of the business world, now in her late forties, had saved Hanson Media from collapse several years back, after her first husband, George Hanson, died suddenly. The story went that before she was forced to step in and save the family business, she'd been a trophy wife.

Smart and savvy and strictly professional as she'd been since he met her, Tom had been having trouble seeing her as mere arm candy for a tycoon. But now he'd been granted that amazing smile, he wasn't having trouble anymore.

That face, that smile…

George Hanson had been one lucky man. And so was her current husband, TAKA-Hanson's chairman of the board, Morito Taka.

"I prize honesty," Helen said. "I prize it highly. So I think it's time I repaid your truth with one of my own. I've done my homework on you, Tom. I've known all along about how you lost that trading job, and the price you paid for what you did. I've been interested to see if you'd tell me about it. And now that you have, I'm more certain than ever on this. Other than that one admittedly serious black mark against you—for which you've paid your dues—your record is spotless. I know you'll make a fine addition to my team. I've got no reservations. You're the man for this job."

Tom's heart slammed against his breastbone. Had he

heard right? Had it worked out, after all? The CEO knew the truth.

And she'd hired him anyway.

He held out his hand. Helen took it. They shook.

When he spoke, his voice was firm and level. "I intend to make sure you never regret this decision."

"I believe you," said Helen. "That's another reason you're our new CFO."

Chapter One

The present...

In the humid darkness of a warm June night, a long, black limousine eased up to the curb of a modest brick bungalow in the Chicago suburb of Forest Park.

Inside the luxurious car, Shelly Winston turned to the uncle she'd met for the first time that evening. "Would you like to come in? I could—"

"Sorry." Drake Thatcher, handsome as an old-time movie star, with coal-black hair and eyes to match, waved away her offer before she'd finished making it. "Thanks, Shelly. I really can't. I've got a flight to catch. I want to be touching down at Teterboro two hours from now."

Teterboro. Even Shelly, who didn't travel in exclusive circles, had heard of the New Jersey airport where all the rich people kept their private jets. The Kennedys flew in and out of Teterboro. And of course her long-lost uncle did, too. Drake was rich, after all. At dinner, he'd told her about his bicoastal lifestyle. He owned a penthouse on the Upper East Side, a beachfront estate in Miami and a Century City condo in Southern California.

The dinner Shelly had just enjoyed had been the finest she'd ever tasted. The lobster had been flavored with hyacinth vapor, whatever that was. And the licorice cake she'd devoured for dessert had been topped with a special muscovado sugar. The menu had no prices on it, but she had a feeling the tab and tip together would have taken care of her mortgage payment for the month—her mortgage which wasn't overdue yet. But would be. Soon.

"Thank you, then," she said sincerely. "For the wonderful dinner. And even more, for the lead on that job at TAKA-Hanson. It sounds like just the kind of thing I'm looking for." *Not to mention what I need. Bad.*

Drake pushed a button and the privacy window behind the driver slid up the rest of the way. Then he leaned across the plush seat toward her, bringing with him the smell of expensive aftershave. It was a fine scent, but he'd laid it on a little too heavily.

He pitched his voice to a confidential level. "I mean it, Shelly. You need to get on that tomorrow. Make a move and make it fast. It just so happens you're in luck with this. I got word that the job would be opening up ahead of their HR department. But it'll be snapped up before noon, take my word on it."

"Don't worry. I'll be there waiting when they open the doors."

"Excellent." He patted her shoulder and sat back in his own seat again, taking the heavy cloud of pricey cologne with him.

"Well, I'll let you get going then. I mean it. Thanks so much."

"One more thing...."

"Sure."

He glanced away, then back to her. "It's not a big deal, just...you might be wiser not to mention my name at TAKA-Hanson."

Shelly frowned. "But I don't see—"

Another wave of his well-manicured hand. "Shelly. I'm sure you know that the business world is a cutthroat one. Unfortunately, in the past, I've found myself going head-to-head with more than one top TAKA executive. No, it probably won't make any difference if you mention that I suggested you apply there. But then again, why take a chance of starting out on the wrong foot with them?" His smile was wide and oh-so-charming.

And Shelly had a powerful suspicion that she was being played.

But for what? Her long-lost uncle had asked nothing of her. All he'd done was to take her out for an expensive dinner and give her a terrific lead when she happened to mention she was looking for a job.

She kept it light. "Honestly, Uncle Drake. What could the TAKA-Hanson people possibly have against a wonderful guy like you?"

Drake shrugged. And backed off the point. "Listen. If you feel more comfortable telling the clerks in HR that your uncle suggested you should apply there, go for it." He glanced at his Rolex. "And I've got to get rolling."

"Thanks again."

"Don't mention it. I'm glad we got together. Call me. Soon. I want to hear all about how much you love your new job."

Inside the house, Shelly turned on the air-conditioning. The day had been hotter than usual for early June and the house was stuffy. She'd been doing without air-conditioning over the last couple of unseasonably warm days. It cost money to keep the place cool—even a small house like hers.

But she could afford to splurge on a little cool air tonight. Because tomorrow she was getting that job. It was exactly the kind of top executive assistant position she'd been looking for.

She flopped to the sofa and grabbed a throw pillow to hug. "TAKA-Hanson, here I come!" The cheer in her voice sounded more than a little forced.

But why wouldn't it? All she had was a tip, after all. There were no guarantees. Maybe someone else had an inside track on the position, too. Maybe her uncle had been wrong and there was no position, after all.

The house seemed so empty. She missed Max. A lot.

Shelly tossed the pillow aside and reached for the phone, auto-dialing her mom's number.

"Hello. Winston residence. This is Norma." Norma

Winston had been a librarian for over thirty years. She'd retired five years before, but she still answered the phone in a formal tone.

"Hey, Mom."

"Honey. Hi."

"I know he's asleep, huh?"

"That child." A world full of love was in those two simple words.

"Keeping you busy, is he?"

"I love every minute of it." Six-year-old Max stayed with his grandparents for a month every summer. Shelly's mom and her dad, Doug, loved having him there. And Max loved the time he spent with them. Shelly missed her son. A lot. But she enjoyed the break from single parenthood, too. Especially this year, when she'd been out of work for three months and was starting to get seriously stressed about it.

"Give him a big kiss for me, huh? Tell him I'll call tomorrow."

"You know he'd rather call *you*."

"No kidding." It was Max's latest thing. Memorizing important phone numbers, making the calls himself. "Okay. Have him call about six. I'll be home by then."

"Home by then?" her mother echoed hopefully. "Something come up on the job front?"

"Oh, Mom. Cross your fingers for me and say a little prayer."

"Honey, you know I will."

"I heard about this great job opening up. Just tonight, as a matter of fact. You'll never guess who I heard it from...."

"Someone I know?"

"Uncle Drake."

"Drake…Thatcher?" Her mom sounded as surprised to hear her half brother's name as Shelly had been when she'd picked up the phone and heard his deep, smooth voice on the other end. Norma Winston and Drake moved in completely different circles. They exchanged Christmas cards, but that was about the extent of their keeping in touch.

"He called this afternoon. He was in town, he said, just for the day. He wanted to meet me. He said it was about time."

"Well. I guess so.…" Her mother's voice trailed off. Shelly knew she was wondering what could possibly have inspired her half brother suddenly to take an interest in Shelly, when up until now he'd behaved as if she didn't exist.

"It is kind of strange, huh?" Shelly voiced her doubts. "I mean, him calling up out of the blue like that?"

"No. No, of course it isn't. I think it's…nice. It's never too late to get to know your family."

Shelly smiled again. Her mother was such a sweetie. Norma's father, Bart Thatcher, had divorced Shelly's grandmother and married "up" into a wealthy New York family, leaving his original family behind. Drake was the first child of Bart's second marriage. He'd grown up rich as they come, while Norma had started out with so little. But Shelly's mom had made a good life for herself and held no grudge.

"He took me to dinner," Shelly said. "And when I told him I was looking for a job, he said there was something coming available at TAKA-Hanson. You've heard of Hanson North America, right?"

"Oh, yes." Norma Winston prided herself on staying informed. She took three newspapers: the *Mt. Vernon Register-News*, the *Tribune* and the *New York Times*. She read all three, too.

"Uncle Drake says Hanson Media merged with a giant Japanese company called TAKA Corporation some years back, becoming Hanson North America here in the States. Since then, under the name TAKA-Hanson, the merged company branched out into other things, beyond the media business. Including this way upscale, exclusive hotel chain. I guess Uncle Drake's got an 'in' there or something, though he was pretty vague about how he knew the job would be open."

"But you're excited?"

"Yeah. I am. I have a feeling this is it."

"Well. I *know* it is."

"Mom. That's what I love about you and Dad. You're always so sure good things will happen."

"Because they will," her mother said. And then she laughed. "Nothing but good news ahead."

"I hope you're right."

"Of course I'm right."

Shelly was ready and waiting at the TAKA-Hanson building the next day when the human resources office opened. She turned in her résumé and made it through two tiers of interviews. When asked what brought her to apply at TAKA-Hanson, she played it safe and left her uncle Drake out of it.

"I like what I've heard about the company," she said. It was true. She'd spent two hours on the Internet before bed the night before, researching like crazy, learning all she could about TAKA-Hanson, which had home offices in Chicago and Tokyo. "And it occurred to me I ought to come in and get my résumé on file," she added. "Just in case."

The woman across the desk nodded. "As it happens, your timing is perfect. We've learned this morning that Tom Holloway, CFO in our hospitality division, will be needing a new assistant."

Yes! Inside, Shelly was jumping up and down, doing the happy dance. But when she spoke, it was in her most polished, professional tone. "It sounds like exactly what I'm looking for."

The woman clicked her mouse and frowned at her computer screen. "If you've got time, I'd like to go ahead and send you upstairs now. You'll meet with Verna Reed, the woman you would be replacing."

"I have time. Definitely."

The elevator ride to the top floor seemed to last forever. But the doors slid wide at last and a slim, fiftyish woman was waiting on the other side. "Shelly? I'm Verna. Follow me…."

They went to Verna's desk in a roomy alcove outside a closed door with Tom Holloway's name on it. Verna looked over Shelly's résumé and explained the job duties and asked questions about how Shelly might handle this or that situation. Shelly felt she did well. And she liked Verna, who was friendly and down-to-earth.

"I love this job," Verna confessed. "The money's

great, there's lots of variety—and Tom Holloway is my hands-down favorite as bosses go. But my husband's retiring. You should see the RV he went out and bought. We've always said someday we'd travel together, see America, all that." She cocked her neatly combed head. "Let me see if Tom can spare a minute or two for you right now. What do you say?"

Shelly's heart did a forward roll. *Yes!* "I'd love to meet Tom."

Two minutes later, Verna ushered her into the sunlit corner office. The man behind the wide desk looked up. He had gorgeous blue eyes. "Shelly. Hi." He rose to greet her.

His jacket was nowhere in evidence and his silk shirt, which exactly matched those unforgettable eyes, was rolled to below the elbows. She took the hand he offered. His grip was solid. Strong.

When he released her hand, he gestured toward a nearby chair. She sat.

"Verna seems to think she's already found her replacement." He had a great voice. Deep and firm. Warm. And so…manly.

She grinned then. She just couldn't help it. "I think so. And I really hope you think so, too."

He had her résumé and application up on his computer. "Let me have a look here.…"

She waited, thinking how attractive he was, wondering if she was happy about that or not. Having a hunky boss could be a distraction.

But hey. She could learn to live with that. She could learn, easy.

"Everything seems to be in order here." He sent her an approving glance. "Two years at Southern Illinois University studying business…and until a month ago, you were managing the office at Coffey Fire Alarm, Incorporated?"

"That's right. Life kind of got in the way of my getting my degree." Life in the form of a beautiful baby boy. "And at Coffey, I wanted a promotion. And more money. They were happy with my work—you can see they gave me a great letter of recommendation. But they're a small company. I was running the office for them. That was the best they had to offer."

"So you quit."

"Yes. I loved working at Coffey. But after making several requests for a raise and a promotion, and being told there was nothing available unless I wanted to move over into sales, I felt the job was going nowhere. I wanted to be free to look full-time for something better." She didn't mention the sleepless nights since then, the worry and the guilt. What sensible single mom quit her job when she didn't have another one lined up? At the time she handed in her resignation, she'd felt she just couldn't bear another day in the job that went nowhere. But months without a paycheck had shown her otherwise.

Tom was nodding. Did that mean he liked her answer?

God. Interviews. Like walking through a minefield of handshakes and loaded questions and cordial smiles.

"What brings you to TAKA-Hanson?"

He *would* have to ask that one. She hated to lie. And really, why not just tell him the truth? Her uncle's name was on the tip of her tongue. But with her savings on life support and the perfect job in the palm of her hand, she couldn't do it, couldn't take the risk of losing what she needed so much.

She played it safe and trotted out the same story she'd given the woman down in HR. It seemed to fly.

"You've heard about our hotel project, then?" he asked.

She had. From Drake, when he'd told her about the job. And from her research the night before. "I saw that article in the *Tribune*. The Taka San Francisco will open in the fall, right?"

"A soft opening," he said. "Gives us a chance to work out the kinks. Our grand opening will be in Kyoto, Japan, over the holidays." He was quiet again, studying his computer screen. "I see there's a child."

"Yes. My son, Maxwell. He's going into first grade this year."

"You're not married," he said thoughtfully, his eyes on the monitor. She'd checked *Single* on the application.

She hitched up her chin. "That's right. It's just Max and me."

"I'm guessing your ex-husband has the boy some of the time?"

"There is no ex-husband. In fact, Max's father is not in the picture."

"You're…on your own?"

Irritation made her curt. "Yes." What business was it of his that Max's dad hadn't wanted a kid? "Is that important, somehow?"

He sat back from the computer screen and rested his elbows on the arms of his plush leather chair. "I don't mean to offend you." His sincere tone and direct gaze banished her annoyance.

"You haven't." Or if he had at first, she was over it.

"I only asked about the child's care because I travel. To the west coast and to Kyoto, currently, to keep an eye on construction and development at our flagship sites. I'm gone for several days a month. Sometimes I'll go on my own, but more often than not, I'll need my assistant with me. Will you be able to manage that, with your son to consider?"

Okay, it wouldn't be easy. But she could make it work. Because she had to. "If I have at least twenty-four hours' notice, I can make arrangements for my son's care. And for the next few weeks, it won't be an issue. Max is down in Mount Vernon—that's my hometown. In southern Illinois, not all that far from St. Louis. He's staying with my parents."

Those dreamboat-blue eyes measured her. Did he find her lacking somehow? Did he have doubts that she could handle a demanding job, with travel, *and* take care of her son?

Shelly sat tall. Though her palms felt clammy and her pulse raced, she faked calmness and confidence for all she was worth.

A sweet, open, girl-next-door face, a megawatt smile and a sharp mind. Plus, she took no crap from anyone. Even a prospective boss.

Tom had liked Shelly on sight. Not only did she seem exactly right for the job, there was something… direct about her. Something true. Her handshake was firm, her references good ones. Tom had the feeling he'd be able to count on Shelly Winston, that he'd quickly come to trust her.

Strange, to find himself thinking of trusting someone he'd just met. As a rule, he was more cautious. He'd learned early that it never paid to trust anyone until they'd proved they could be depended on.

Whatever. The point was, she seemed competent. Quick on the uptake and qualified.

He was damned relieved to find someone so quickly. If he had to lose efficient, dependable Verna, his assistant since he'd come to TAKA-Hanson, at least it was looking as though he had her replacement lined up.

He scrolled through the paperwork once more. Everything seemed in order. All he had to do was give the final okay and HR would confirm her references. By tomorrow, Verna would be showing her the ropes.

"It says here you can start right away...."

She beamed him that beautiful smile. "The sooner the better, as far as I'm concerned."

"Mom. You can tell me. Are you missing me too much?" Max used his most serious voice.

"Yes," she said, hugging the phone to her shoulder, wishing he was there so she could hug him in person. "I miss you more than words can ever say."

"You don't need me to come home or anything, do you?"

"Do you want to come home?"

He hesitated. "Uh. Well…"

She smiled to herself. "I think you mean no."

"Well. I'm having a whole lot of fun, that's all. But I'll come home if you need me."

"You stay right there. And don't worry. I'll be fine. I promise. Tell me about what you've been up to with Granny and Grandpa?"

"I caught two frogs down at the creek today."

"Big ones?"

"Yep." Her parents had two acres. A small stream ran about a thousand yards behind the house. "Granny let me keep them in a jar. I even punched holes in the top so that they can breathe. But I only get to keep them for a day, she said. I have to let them go so they can eat a lot of flies. I caught some pollywogs, too. One has legs. I want to watch it turn into a frog, but that takes time, Granny says. And Grandpa took me to get ice cream yesterday. I had vanilla. I like vanilla…."

He babbled away, intent on sharing each small, special detail of his summer at his grandma's house. Shelly listened and made admiring, interested noises at the right moments, all the while picturing his pointy little chin and his thick, unruly wheat-colored hair. One big cowlick, that hair of his. It stuck up from his head even when she tried to comb it down.

She wondered if he'd lost his glasses again, or broken them. The thought brought another grin. She could afford to grin over broken glasses now. She had a job. They'd be calling to tell her she was hired tomorrow. She just knew they would. Tom had as good as said she was hired, though the formal offer had yet to be made.

Finally, Max ran out of steam. "And that's all. I'm having fun, like I said. And I'm being good. And I had a little problem with my glasses when I left them in Grandpa's chair and he sat on them. But it's okay. Granny taped them up good as new."

"I'm sure she did." She made a mental note to call the optometrist and have another pair made. "I love you."

"Love you, too. I think I better call you again. I think it should be soon. You know, so you won't have to miss me too much."

She suggested Saturday and named a time.

"Okay. I'll call you then. Granny's here to talk to you now...."

Norma didn't bother with hellos. She went straight for, "Well? How did it go?"

"Really good, Mom."

"You got the job?" Her mother sounded almost as excited as Shelly felt.

"I think so. I should know for sure tomorrow."

"I just know this is it, honey."

"Oh, Mom. I hope you're right."

"Of course I'm right. You're going to get that job."

Shelly hardly slept that night. She couldn't wait for morning and the phone call she felt certain was coming. She was up at six, dressed and ready to take on the world by a quarter of seven.

Too keyed up to eat, she sat at the two-person table in her small kitchen, staring at the phone in front of her, drinking cup after cup of strong, black coffee.

Nine o'clock went by. Ten. Ten-thirty...

At ten after eleven, the damn thing finally rang.

Shelly jumped in surprise and then gaped at it, hardly daring to believe, almost afraid to answer for fear it would be some telemarketer or a friend from her old job calling to ask how she'd been doing.

She let it ring twice, just to prove that she could, and then she snatched it up in the middle of the third ring. "Hello?"

"Shelly Winston, please." It was one of the women from TAKA-Hanson HR.

Shelly spoke with great poise as she accepted the job. With amazing composure, considering the fact that she could now do miraculous things: pay her mortgage, order new glasses for Max, head over to Dominick's and buy herself a fat filet mignon, and not care in the least that it was seventeen dollars a pound. "I'll be at the office tomorrow at nine. Goodbye." She hung up the phone.

And then she ran around the house yelling, "Yes, yes, yes, yes!"

Once she'd finished shouting out her joy, she called her mother and basked in Norma's pleasure and praise. Before she hung up, her mom said, "When you call your uncle to thank him, thank him for me, too."

"I will, Mom."

Drake. She certainly did owe him a big, fat thank-you. She called. And got his voice mail.

"Uncle Drake. It's Shelly. I just want to thank you. I got that job at TAKA-Hanson. I can't tell you how much this means to me. Thank you...." She let out a self-conscious laugh. "But I guess I said that already. Oh. And my mom says thank you, too...."

What else? She couldn't think of anything. She said goodbye and hung up.

After that, she got out all her unpaid bills and wrote the checks, addressed and stamped the envelopes and put them in the mail. Because she could. Then she went to the store and bought groceries, including a small, beautiful, way-too-expensive filet mignon. She also applied for a passport. And since she would probably be needing it soon, she paid extra to get it fast.

The afternoon went by in a warm glow of anticipation for the job she just knew she was going to love.

Shelly did love her new job.

And she really liked her new boss. Truthfully, she liked Tom a little *too* much, and she knew it. There was just something about him—beyond his good looks and strong handshake, his sense of humor and that tempting aura of power and command he wore so confidently. There were…shadows behind his eyes. Though he never came across as brooding or sad, she still had a feeling he'd been through tough times—and come out a better man for them.

She constantly reminded herself that a *feeling* was not reality. He'd probably been born into privilege. And if he'd suffered, it had been over whether to go to Harvard or Yale.

Yes, she liked him. And she was attracted to him. But so what? Nothing was going to come of it. She was there to work, not to get involved with the boss.

On her fifth day on the job, Verna announced she was leaving a week earlier than she'd planned.

"After all," the older woman said. "No point in

having the two of us in each other's hair when it's perfectly clear to me you can handle everything just fine on your own. I'm going to talk to Tom about this right now. I'm thinking I'll finish out the week on call. I'll be out of your way, but you can give me a buzz if necessary. Monday, you're on your own. And Hank and I will hit the road. What do you say to that?"

"I say I really hate to see you go…"

Verna laughed. "But you can't wait for the chance to have this desk to yourself. Well, it's all yours. Starting tomorrow, I'm outta here."

The phone was ringing when Shelly got home that night. She raced in the door and grabbed it on the fourth ring, just before her machine picked up.

It was her uncle Drake. "I hear you're exceeding expectations at that new job of yours."

"How do you know so much?"

"I thought I explained that. There are always ways…" Which explained exactly nothing.

"Uncle Drake, I'm starting to think you have spies at TAKA-Hanson." She said the words jokingly, even though she had a feeling he did have spies at the company. He would have to, wouldn't he, to have known about her job before anyone else did, to have found out that she was doing well when she'd been there a week and was still, technically at least, a trainee?

He went on as if she hadn't spoken. "Assistant to the CFO, hospitality division. I like the sound of that."

"Me, too." She reminded herself that she ought to be grateful to him. She *was* grateful to him. "And seriously.

I love this job. It's exactly what I was hoping to find. And thanks to you, I did find it. I can't tell you how much I appreciate your mentioning that it might become available."

"Glad to help. Now, I want you to get good and settled in. Prove yourself trustworthy. That's important. Next time I'm in Chicago, we'll have dinner again. We'll talk. I might have a favor or two to ask by then."

Alarm jangled through her. Was her long-lost uncle setting her up somehow? For what?

Cautiously, she asked, "What kind of favor are we talking about here?"

"No need to get ahead of ourselves."

"But I really would like to know. You keep hinting that there's something I can do for you, but you never—"

"Well, I was thinking along the lines of a little… information gathering. As Holloway's assistant, you'll have access to certain sensitive material I can't get any other way."

"Access to what, exactly?"

"Later. Right now, you only need to do your new job and do it well."

"Uncle Drake, are you telling me you want to spy for you?"

She heard him sigh. "We're getting ahead of ourselves, don't you think?"

"No, I don't. I need to know specifically what you're going to expect me to—"

Again he interrupted her. "Don't worry, Shelly. I just wanted to congratulate you and tell you to keep up the good work. I'll call you. Soon."

Before she could say another word, she heard the click on the other end. He'd hung up. She set the phone down carefully and tried to decide what she ought to do next.

Call him back and demand specifics? She knew already what she'd get for that. He'd tell her again not to worry.

Should she call her mom, ask for advice? No. It wasn't her mom's problem and she didn't want to worry her.

But the situation made her nervous. Her uncle, who'd spent most of his life behaving as if her branch of the family didn't exist, showed up out of nowhere, wined and dined her and then told her where to go and what to do to get the kind of job she'd been seeking for months with zero success.

It was too perfect. Add his warning that she shouldn't mention him at TAKA-Hanson? Definitely suspicious. And now he'd told her right out that in time he would want her to spy for him.

But so what? She'd done nothing wrong. She *would* do nothing wrong.

And until her uncle actually asked her to do something unethical, she would mind her own business and not borrow trouble.

Chapter Two

The next day, Shelly claimed Verna's desk for her own. She got to work at seven-thirty and set up the computer the way she liked it. She went through the desk drawers and rearranged them to her personal satisfaction.

Tom arrived at eight-fifteen. "First day flying solo, huh?" He wore a designer suit and a tie that matched his eyes and she thought he looked amazing.

"I've got Verna's cell on auto-dial if I need her. Which I won't."

"Confidence. I like that." He looked at her with admiration. She resisted the urge to smooth her hair. "Give me fifteen minutes and we'll go over the calendar."

"Will do."

He disappeared into his office and she stared at the place he'd been, grinning like a fool.

Note to self: mind on the job, not on the boss....

The day progressed without a single crisis—not on Shelly's end, anyway. She put the final touches on the arrangements for Verna's retirement party, which she'd managed to move up to tomorrow night after Verna had confided that her husband wanted to head for some RV park in Ohio on Sunday.

Tom spent most of his day putting out fires.

He had to call an emergency meeting about the San Francisco flagship site. The hotel was supposed to be opening in September and the interiors, according to the site manager there, were a disaster. The designer was not only over budget, but also behind schedule. *Way* behind schedule.

There was also some problem at the Kyoto site. The facility there was still under construction, and things had been moving right along until the past few weeks. And there were accounting issues, as well. Tom took another long meeting with his managers to discuss the situation.

Friday he told Shelly he would be going to San Francisco on Monday and then to Japan on Thursday. "You'll probably have to move a few meetings around for me. Go over my appointments and make the calls. Push everything to the following week, if you can. We should have the day here in Chicago on Wednesday, so you can pack it with whatever can't be put off till the week of the thirtieth. Let me know if there are issues."

"Yes. Of course."

He said, "And I'd like you with me for both trips."

With him...

Somehow, Shelly managed not to jump up and down in her chair. This was the life. Jetting to the west coast. Zipping off to Japan...

She'd get packed over the weekend. It was going to be fabulous. She needed a decent suitcase. One of those new ones with four wheels. She'd pick one up Saturday morning. They couldn't be *that* expensive, could they?

He asked, "Can you manage it?"

"It?" She blinked.

"Two trips in one week?"

"Uh. Yeah. I can. I'm with you. No biggie." Max would still be in Mount Vernon next week. Childcare wouldn't be a problem. Not this time.

"Got a passport?"

"Yes, I do. I took care of that on the day I got the job."

"Good. What else? Everything under control for Verna's party tonight?"

"Everything's a go. I just got off the phone with the caterer. And I checked around the office to make certain they all knew we'd changed the date. From the responses I got, we should have a great turnout."

They held Verna's retirement party in a friendly little bar on a side street, a few blocks west of the office. Most of the women from HR were there, along with the lower-level executives from the finance department and several of the secretaries and assistants Verna had worked with in her twenty-two years at Hanson Media, then TAKA-Hanson.

Verna's husband, Hank, came, too. And Tom, of course.

The beer flowed freely and the food was cafeteria-style, set out in chafing dishes on a long table. Customers grabbed a plate and helped themselves.

Verna got a Rolex to mark the occasion and Tom gave a little speech in her honor. And he offered a toast. "To Verna. We'll miss you. Think about us now and then while you and Hank are out there seeing America...." He raised his beer glass to his former assistant as Hank put his arm around her and kissed the top of her graying head. Everybody clapped and cheered.

From the stool she'd claimed down the bar, Shelly raised her glass high and joined in the toast, happy for Verna, even happier for herself.

Someone tapped her shoulder. She swiveled her chair around. "Hey, Lil." Lillian Todd worked for one of the finance managers. She had sleek red hair and a killer body. She seemed to spend most of her time in the break room and making the rounds, chatting up all the secretaries, flirting with every guy in sight. Verna had confided in Shelly that it was lucky for Lil she was as smart as she was sexy. She spent so much time gossiping and making eyes at the men, she needed to be fast to get her work done, too.

"Doing all right on your own?" Lil had to shout to be heard over the rowdy crowd.

Shelly nodded, and shouted back, "So far, so good." Lillian opened her mouth to say something else—but then she blinked and aimed her sexiest smile at a point past Shelly's shoulder.

"Terrific party." The male voice, deep and warm and threaded with humor, spoke in Shelly's ear.

Tom. She turned to him—and tried not to get lost in those baby blues of his, tried not to sigh over the way his eyes crinkled at the corners, over the five-o'clock shadow on his manly jaw. His suit jacket, as usual, was nowhere in evidence. His tie was gone, too. He'd rolled his shirtsleeves the way he liked to do.

The strangest feeling washed through her. A mix of excitement—and tenderness.

Tenderness? For a man she'd known less than two weeks? That hardly seemed possible. Yet somehow, it *was* so.

The party seemed to get louder by the minute. She had to lean close or shout. She leaned. "Having fun?"

"You bet."

Someone in the corner let out a whoop and everyone started laughing and clapping again. It simply wasn't the kind of party where you could have an actual conversation.

So she nodded and sipped her beer and stared into those eyes of his. They actually twinkled. Funny. Until Tom, she'd thought that twinkling eyes were more a figure of speech than anything that occurred in nature.

He leaned toward her again. She met him halfway. He smelled of some subtle aftershave and soap. And man. All man.

"Hungry?" He set his empty glass on the bar.

She set hers beside it. He gestured toward the table with the food on it and she slid off her stool and started walking, aware with every step that he followed. They filled a couple of plates and went back to the bar.

Since it was such a chore to try to talk, they ate to the rowdy laughter of their coworkers and the occasional shouted good wishes directed at Verna and Hank.

Shelly had hired a DJ and the place had a postage stamp of a dance floor at one end. Hank gave the DJ a big tip and a list of favorite tunes. Then he pulled Verna onto the floor. They swayed to the music. A few other couples joined them. Not too many. There wasn't that much room.

Shelly watched, feeling sentimental. Hank and Verna reminded her a little of her parents: married forever, still going strong.

Tom leaned close again. "Dance?"

She slanted him a look—wanting the dance, wondering if they were carrying this a little too far. For the umpteenth time, she reminded herself that the last thing she needed was an office romance.

Especially one with her boss.

Even if he did have the bluest eyes in Chicagoland.

But then again, it was just a dance. No big deal....

He held out his hand. She settled the light chain strap of her bag more securely on her shoulder and put her hand in his. His lean fingers closed around hers. Warm. Strong. Good.

Too good.

It was another slow one. Hank seemed to have picked all slow ones. A real romantic, that Hank.

Tom pulled her into his arms. Shelly tucked herself into him—not too close, just enough that she could feel his body's signals as he led her.

Neither of them said a word. That suited Shelly just fine. It was...lovely. A few brief moments out of time. One hand enclosed hers, the other fitted itself possessively on the curve of her lower back. Shelly closed her eyes and cleared her mind of thought, enjoying the sweet strains of the old, romantic song. And even better than the music was the heat of Tom's body, so close to hers, the light caress of his big hand at her back, the occasional rough brush of his cheek against her temple.

It was over much too soon. A fast number came on next.

Hank groaned, "What about my list? That one's not on my list."

Everybody laughed, more of them crowding forward onto the floor, fast-dancing to the heavy rock beat of the new song.

Tom dropped his hand from her back. But he didn't let her go. The fingers of his other hand stayed firmly wrapped around hers. He led her off the floor.

She was far too content with going wherever he felt like taking her. Not smart, and she knew it. Professionally speaking, she really ought to break up this twosome they somehow seemed to have formed. It was one thing to spend a little social time with her boss.

And something else altogether when it started feeling like a date, when she found herself imagining what it might be like to kiss him, to walk down a summer street in the heat of the evening, holding hands with him. To…

Uh-uh. Enough. Not going there. No way.

She slowed her steps and gently pulled her hand free of his. He turned back to her with a questioning frown.

"Ladies' room." She mouthed the words and stuck a thumb back over her shoulder.

He shrugged and nodded.

She turned and left him, quickly, before she found some excuse to stay.

In the ladies' room, she freshened her lip gloss and brushed her hair. It didn't take long. But if she went back out too soon, Tom could be waiting where she'd left him.

She entered a stall, feeling kind of silly, but wanting to give Tom plenty of time to find someone else to hang with. When it finally got too ridiculous just standing in there, she emerged and washed her hands.

As she was reaching for a towel, Lil came out of one of the other stalls.

"Hey, Shel. Havin' *fun?*" She put the oddest emphasis on the word *fun*.

Was it some kind of dig? But the other assistant met her eyes in the mirror, a friendly smile on those plump red lips.

"Yeah," Shelly said. "I am. A real good time. You?"

"Fabulous."

Out in the bar, the party was still in full swing. Shelly caught sight of Tom, over at a corner table with some of the other execs from the finance department and a couple of guys she was pretty sure were from down in accounting. She started to turn and go the other way, but Tom spotted her and signaled her over.

She went to him, aware of a rising feeling in her chest, wishing she wasn't so glad that he'd caught her before she made her escape. The others made room for her, leaving the chair beside him empty.

Shelley sat down next to her boss.

"I was beginning to wonder if someone had kidnapped you." He leaned close as he spoke to her, though he didn't really need to.

The noise level seemed to have faded down a few notches in the last half hour or so. The bar wasn't so crowded. People had left to catch their trains home, and those that remained talked more quietly—over at the bar, and around the tables.

She smiled at him, her widest, warmest smile. "Nope. Not kidnapped. Right here, safe and sound."

"It's a relief. I can't afford to lose another assistant. I might not be so lucky next time finding a replacement."

They looked at each other, the eye contact drawing out longer than she should have allowed it to.

Then Jessica Valdez, one of Tom's managers, brought up the interior-design issues they were having at The Taka San Francisco. The rest of them started talking at once—offering complaints, suggestions and even a few solutions. The guys from accounting really got into it. Riki, the internationally acclaimed designer, was on everyone's bad side.

"Never trust a guy without a last name," grumbled one of the accountants.

"Maybe Riki *is* his last name," joked a junior finance exec.

"Two names," said one of the finance managers. "A guy should have two names. First and last. It's fiscally irresponsible to try getting along with one. Not to mention damned pretentious."

Tom called a halt to the subject after a while. "I know it's an issue. And *you* all know I'll be dealing with Riki face-to-face on Monday. And Thursday, I'll get with Robby." Robby Axelrod was in charge of construction on the Kyoto site. "See what we can do about the cost problems there."

A few minutes later, Verna and Hank came over to say goodbye. Shelly got up and gave Verna a hug. "Send me a postcard."

Verna grinned. "I promise. I'll keep in touch. And thanks for the party. It was terrific."

Tom got up, too, and walked the couple to the door of the bar. When he came back to the table, everyone else started making going-home noises.

Since Shelly had taken charge of the party when she moved up the date, she went ahead and played hostess. She stuck around till the last stragglers called it a night. Finally, she flipped out her shiny new TAKA-Hanson credit card and paid the tab.

Tom took the padded bench in the vestibule and waited for Shelly to head for the door.

She seemed surprised to see him there. "Hey. You didn't have to wait."

He rose. "Can't have my favorite assistant wandering out onto Clark Street alone."

She gave him a laugh. He really liked her laugh. "I think it's totally safe, Tom."

"You never know."

She lifted her slim wrist and glanced at her watch. "It's not even nine."

"Almost dark. Could be dangerous."

"The biggest danger isn't the kind you can protect me from." Her brandy-colored eyes teased him.

He took her arm and turned her for the door. "Tell me all about it."

"Michigan Avenue. It's in walking distance and I've got plastic. Blocks and blocks of great stores. I could end up spending a whole lot of money I don't even have."

"So I swear I won't take you shopping. Whew. Another bankruptcy averted. Aren't you glad I'm here?"

She smiled again. He loved her smile. "Okay. I'm glad. Happy now?" She looked worried, suddenly. "Where's your jacket?"

"You're a hell of an assistant. Nothing gets by you."

"If someone's walked off with your suit coat..."

"I left it—along with my tie—at the office." He guided her through the door into the warmth of the evening. "Nice out." He kept her hand wrapped around his arm and headed north on Clark, for no other reason than that staying on the move seemed a good way to keep her with him.

They were going to be working closely together from now on and it never hurt to get a little social time with his assistant. No, he'd never walked arm-in-arm up Clark Street with Verna. But then, Verna was fifty-four and happily married. Different assistant, different approach.

Tom wanted to know more about Shelly. That seemed perfectly reasonable to him. He liked her and she was a colleague, a colleague who interested him. A lot.

In no time, they'd reached Washington Square. They walked around the park, admiring the elaborate masonry buildings erected by Chicago's elite after the famous fire at the end of the nineteenth century. Then he led her on the path that ran diagonally through the center of the square.

He said, "I thought we ought to get to know each other better."

She paused on the concrete walk. "How well is 'better'?"

"Well, I don't know. Better than we know each other now." He guided her forward a few steps.

But she only stopped again and pulled her arm from his. They stood exactly in the middle of the square of park, facing each other. "I want this job, Tom. I love it already."

"Good."

"And I need it. I don't want to do anything that could potentially screw it up."

"I don't see how you could screw it up. You're very good, Shelly. Smart. Efficient. With strong office skills."

"I'm not talking about how good I am at my job."

Tom gave up finessing her. He looked at her steadily. "Of course you're not."

She caught her lower lip between her pretty white teeth. "I… This is so awkward. And I'm scared that you're going to get offended—or worse."

"I'm not. I promise you."

She laughed, a nervous sound. "Men do, you know?"

He wanted to touch her. But he kept his hands to himself. "Not me."

She pressed those soft lips together and nodded. "Well. Good. Sometimes…office romances work out fine." She spoke slowly. Thoughtfully. "But sometimes—probably more often than not—they end with someone hurt. Or someone angry. Then working together becomes too difficult. I can't have that happen. I really can't."

He got the message. Loud and clear. It was a reasonable argument, and he could understand her fears. He wanted to tell her not to worry, that no matter what, she wouldn't lose her job as his assistant. But he had no right to promise such a thing. In the end, there really were no guarantees.

"Come on." He touched her arm, but didn't take it. She went with him the rest of the way through the park to a row of iron benches on the edge of the square, facing the imposing facade of the Newberry Library.

For a while they just sat there. Tom let the silence spin out. It was full dark by then, the streetlights blooming bright, the fountain in front of the library bubbling away, making those happy splashing sounds as the water shot upward and tumbled back into the fountain's bowl. An old couple strolled past, the man frailer than the woman. He held her arm and leaned heavily on a cane. And there were others, most walking fast, in a hurry to get wherever they were going.

"You live in Forest Park, right?" he asked after a while.

She sent him a glance.

He put up both hands. "Don't shoot me. It was on your résumé."

An unwilling smile broke across those full lips. She shook her head. "Do you ever give up?"

"Persistence. Key to success. Tell me about your place."

"Tom…"

"Come on. It's getting-to-know-you time. Totally innocent."

"Hah."

She had him pegged. It wasn't innocent. Tom knew that. Not innocent in the least. He was drawn to Shelly. Powerfully. She made him want to take the kind of chances he'd long ago stopped taking.

He knew he should respect the boundaries she'd just set. But when he looked into those brown eyes of hers, well, what he *should* be doing seemed of no importance.

"About your place…?"

She blew out a breath. "Oh, all right. It's got three bedrooms and two baths. My parents helped me buy it. It's small, but it's mine." She turned to him. In the glow of the streetlamp a few feet away, her eyes were dark velvet and her skin shone like pearls.

Tom smiled to himself. He knew she liked him. Maybe more than she wanted to like him. He'd take it a day at a time. Anything might happen.

As a rule, he would never consider seducing his secretary. But he *was* considering it. More than considering it. It felt…right, somehow, with Shelly. He wanted her. *And* he liked her. That seemed a rare thing to him. As each day passed, Tom was only more certain that, between him and Shelly, the rules didn't apply.

She said, "You realize I know almost nothing about *you*."

"Is that an accusation?"

She sighed. "Well, yeah. I guess it is. Where do *you* live?"

"I've got a great condo on East Randolph."

"Right in the Loop." The Loop was downtown, so named because the train system looped in a circle around it. Living space there was at a premium. She went on, "I might have guessed. And you can see Grant Park from your balcony, right?"

"Yeah. I can see it." He nudged her with his elbow. Gently.

She shot him a wary glance. "What?"

"We could go there right now. I'll show you my... view."

She laughed. "I think you're dangerous."

"Who, me?" He did his best to look harmless.

"Let me guess. You're from somewhere back east. You went to Yale. You were on the rowing team..."

"Princeton. Coxswain, heavyweight men's crew. I had a full ride."

"In the rowboat?"

He chuckled. "I meant scholarships. They covered everything, tuition, fees, living expenses. I never would have gotten near the Ivy League otherwise."

A frown crinkled her smooth forehead. "Not from a rich family? Not from Pennsylvania or Massachusetts or upstate New York?"

"I was born and raised in Tulsa, Oklahoma. My dad was a janitor and my mom worked in a dentist's office. They were older. My mom was forty-five when she had me. I was their only kid."

"Was?"

"Yeah. They died years ago. My dad went first. Heart attack. My mom followed not long after." He didn't say the rest, that the stress of his arrest and the trial for insider trading had really taken it out of them. Dan Holloway died while Tom was in prison. Tom got out in time to be at his mother's bedside when she went.

Shelly's big brown eyes were soft. "Wow. That's tough. How old were you when you lost them?"

"Twenty-four."

"I can't imagine getting along without my parents." She put her hand on his arm. It felt damn good there. Warm. And steady. "I'm sorry, Tom."

He looked into her eyes and felt like a fraud. *They died because I broke their hearts....*

He had the craziest urge right then, to tell her everything. All the gory details. His apprenticeship in greed, ambition and corruption under a master manipulator, his long free fall from grace.

It was an urge he had little trouble resisting. He wasn't going there. He liked Shelly. He wanted to get to know her better. A *lot* better.

But some ugly stories were better left unshared.

He lowered his arm from under her touch. "You do what you have to do. I went into the army after they died."

"Time for a change, huh?"

"You could say that. When I got out, I got my MBA on the GI bill from the University of Texas. I worked in Dallas and Atlanta, then Dallas again. And then back to New York. And now Chicago."

"Back?"

"Excuse me?"

"You said you went *back* to New York...."

Way to blow it, Holloway. He tried to act casual as

he covered his ass. "I had a job in New York before my parents died." And he went right on before she had a chance to ask him what kind of job. "What else? My favorite color is orange and I'm becoming a Cubs fan. I hate Thai food, love Italian. Two serious relationships."

"Marriages, you mean?"

"Uh-uh. Never went that far. Now you. Come on. It's only fair. Favorite color?"

"I love blue."

"And about the Cubs?"

"The Cubs are tops with me. I like Thai food, like Italian better. I have a thing about tuna fish. Love it."

"A little mercury. What's the harm?"

"Exactly. Never been married, either—and I see those questions in your eyes."

"Busted. Your son's father…?"

"Okay. Since I feel like we're *almost* friends—in a strictly professional way…"

He made a circular, move-it-along motion with his hand. "Yeah?"

"I got pregnant in college. The boy didn't want anything to do with being a dad. He agreed to sign papers giving up his rights to Max. I haven't seen him since."

"That's cold. Signing away your own kid."

She shifted on the bench, turning her body toward him. "Honestly, I'm not bitter." She looked so…earnest. And damn it, he wanted to slide his fingers under her hair, hook his hand around her neck and pull her close for a kiss.

But he played fair—for now—and held himself in check. "I like your attitude, Winston."

"Hey. Thanks."

There was one of those moments. The fountain across the street burbled away and people hurried past a few feet from the bench and Tom and Shelly grinned at each other like a couple of lovestruck fools.

Lovestruck…

Strange choice of words. Yeah, he liked her. He *wanted* her. But it was way early to be using the word *love*.

He made himself break the eye contact.

After a few seconds, she said, "It's worked out all right for me and Max. It…wasn't meant to be, between Max's dad and me. And Max is smart and funny and happy. And loving. He doesn't need a dad who's not one hundred percent there for him."

"I want to meet this kid."

"Just don't give him your phone number."

"What?"

She laughed. "Oh, nothing. It's his thing lately. He's discovered the wonder of the telephone. He likes to make phone calls—you know, dial the number all by himself—and then talk your ear off."

Tom grinned. "Definitely. Need to meet him."

"Well, he's with his grandparents until the first of July. So you'll just have to wait." She rose before he could reach out a hand and stop her. "This has been great, Tom.…"

He resisted the strong urge to grab her hand, to hold on until she sat back down beside him.

With a shrug, he stood. "At least I know your favorite color now."

She tipped her chin up to meet his gaze. The fountain

lights made those brown eyes of hers gleam golden. "Yeah. Top priority. Knowing that your secretary loves blue."

"You never know when information like that will come in handy."

"Oh. Right." Her voice was breathy. In spite of her insistence that she wouldn't get involved with him, her eyes begged for a kiss. "And that I like Italian food. That's so important…."

Her full lips tempted him. One kiss. What could it really hurt? Two kisses. Three.

A night full of kisses. He wanted that. With this woman. He wanted it bad.

Time to hail a cab. He saw one coming and raised a hand. The cab slowed and stopped at the curb.

Two steps and Tom was pulling open the door. He gestured her in.

She hung back. "Uh. No. Really, I'll just catch the train. It's no problem."

"Shelly. Get in."

Chapter Three

"Four hundred East Randolph," Tom told the driver as the cab pulled away from the curb. He turned to Shelly. "He'll take you home from there."

"Great. Thanks." Shelly stared out the smeared window on her side of the cab.

Traffic was relatively light. In no time they were sailing down Michigan Avenue, turning onto East Randolph....

The cab pulled up to the curb in front of a high-rise.

Tom sent her a glance and a nod. "See you Monday, then." He knocked on the partition. The cabby slid it open and Tom handed some bills through. "Take her to Forest Park."

The cabby smiled. "Sure, man."

"Thank you." Shelly spoke softly.

Tom gave her a last smile. "Don't be late for the flight."

"I'm never late."

"I noticed." He pushed open his door and he was gone.

The cabby said, "Where to in Forest Park?"

She gave him her address. The ride home took a half hour. She spent most of that time telling herself she wasn't disappointed in the least that he hadn't tried to lure her up to his apartment.

The flight to San Francisco was commercial, first class. Nonstop. And on time. They left the ground at 7:20.

Tom spent an hour or so going over spreadsheets and answering e-mails. Shelly caught up on some letters Tom wanted in the mail by Wednesday and listened to her Fast and Easy Japanese CD, which she'd copied to her iPod, in preparation for the trip to Kyoto on Thursday.

At eight-thirty Chicago time, Tom shut his computer down. Shelly took off her earbuds and put her iPod away.

"Breakfast?" he asked.

"Please."

He hadn't said a word about Friday night. Since she'd met him at the gate at six, he'd been friendly in a strictly business kind of way.

That was great with Shelly—just great. Or so she kept telling herself.

They ate bacon and asparagus frittata, croissants and excellent coffee. First class, she was discovering, not only had roomy, comfortable seats, but also better food than you got when you went coach.

He briefed her on Riki, the world-famous designer who was way behind schedule on the fabulous interiors at The Taka, SF.

"Riki's got the credentials," Tom said. "He's done the mansions of some of the biggest names in the business world. And he's designed hotel interiors before. High-end boutique-style hotels. Even a small chain. He hasn't done anything on this scale up till now, but he came to us highly recommended and his plan for the project was just what we wanted. We're not getting why he's messing up so damn bad now."

"Riki. I swear I've heard of him. Did he ever have a TV show?"

Tom nodded. "*Million Dollar Design.* He's still doing it. Syndicated. Interior design for the rich and famous—mostly high-level money men, Donald–Trump types."

"Very tall, very thin—with red hair combed into a swoosh at the top of his head?"

"That's Riki."

"The times I saw the show, he really laid on the drama. Yelling at people, treating every setback like the end of the world."

"That's just his act for the cameras. It plays well. Viewers love a train wreck—one he always pulls out of at the end, with everybody happy and another rich executive living in his dream house."

"I guess...."

"But behind the scenes, Riki's strictly professional.

At least in terms of his behavior. And his designs are amazing. Too bad he's not getting the job done. At this rate, we'll be putting off the September opening. And that can't happen."

"What will you do, replace him?"

"I'm hoping it doesn't have to come to that."

Speaking of luxury hotels…

The one they stayed in was downtown. Shelly's room had a gorgeous view of the bay, a bed like a cloud, a flat-panel television and an open shower. She unpacked quickly and met Tom in the lobby.

Outside, the streets were steep, the sun shining and the temperature in the high sixties. The air smelled of the sea, which surrounded the city on all sides.

Shelly heard the charming ring of a cable-car bell as they ducked into a cab. It was a short ride to The Taka, which looked pretty fantastic from the outside: twenty-five stories of silver-gray granite and sparkling glass.

Inside, things weren't so good. It was all soaring, empty spaces, without furniture or fixtures. They walked on sub-flooring—no carpets, no marble.

Riki was waiting for them in his office on the second floor. Topping seven feet, wearing a bamboo-green silk shirt and a scarf around his neck, his trademark swoosh of red hair rising like a wave from the top of his head, the famous designer was polite and subdued. And very concerned about the lack of progress on the interiors.

The meeting lasted the rest of the day and included an extensive tour of the facility, where they got to get up-close and personal with all that wasn't getting done.

Shelly took notes, as Tom had asked her to do. Riki had reasons. A whole lot of reasons why it had been impossible for him to stay on schedule.

The carpets were his own design. But the supplier had problems with the dyes. They'd had to start over twice. And the lighting fixtures were on order. Yes, they were weeks late in being delivered, but they were coming. They were promised for a week from today. Absolutely. No more delays....

It went on like that. Through the furnishings and the flooring, the bathroom fixtures and the specially made pillowtop beds, the three-thousand-thread-count sheets, the Egyptian-cotton bath towels. Even the window treatments had issues.

But Riki assured them he was pulling it together. He had spreadsheets and schedules that proved, he said, he'd be exactly where he should be within a month's time.

"That's cutting it pretty damn close," said Tom.

"But my original schedule had a lot of room for just these kinds of delays. So as you can see, we're going to be ready in plenty of time."

Tom looked at him levelly. "I can give you only so much leeway, Riki. You have to know that."

"Count on me. You know you can."

That night, Riki took them to dinner at Fleur de Lys, the world-famous restaurant, where thick draperies adorned the ceiling and the wine was excellent and flowed a little too freely. The food was wonderful.

Riki saw them into a cab at quarter after ten. "I'm determined," he said before waving them off, "to get everything back on track within the time frame I laid out for you."

Tom shook his hand.

The ride back to the hotel was a quiet one. Tom seemed lost in thought.

They pulled up to the hotel entrance and he turned to her. Every time she looked in his eyes she remembered why blue was her favorite color.

He said, "You want to see Fisherman's Wharf?"

All the reasons they shouldn't do social things together raced through her mind. But how many times had she seen San Francisco? That would be never. This was her first time in the city by the bay. Chances were she'd visit again, now she worked with Tom.

But you never knew what the future might bring.

Shelly let her smile bloom wide. "I thought you'd never ask."

"It's a total tourist trap," Tom said, when they stood at the rail on Pier 39 and admired the sea lions.

"Still." The brisk wind off the bay blew her hair across her cheeks. She smoothed it back behind her ears. Not that it stayed there. "It's Fisherman's Wharf. And now I can say I've been here…"

He had his jacket off—as usual—and he carried it hooked on a finger, slung back over his shoulder. He'd loosened his tie. The wind whipped at his hair. Even at almost eleven at night, the lights were bright and people milled around them and the smell of steaming crab from a street vendor scented the air.

"Okay," Tom admitted with a grin. "It is kind of cool."

She laughed. "Cool? It's freezing." She shivered. He offered his coat and she took it gladly, wrapping it around her like a cape, letting the arms hang free.

As the sea lions barked for tidbits from the tourists that lined the rail, Tom edged in closer and turned her toward the open water. She was enjoying herself far too much—enjoying all of it: the warmth of his hands on her shoulders, the feel of him close at her back, the cozy comfort of his jacked wrapped around her.

He said, "That's Alcatraz, on the left." By the glow of the moon and the lights on the island, she could see the famous prison quite clearly. He added, "Angel Island is right there beside it."

Shelly got out her cell and took a few pictures. Then they strolled around a while. He didn't take her hand, or wrap an arm around her. She tried not to wish that he would.

They found a free bench and sat down and she was reminded of Friday night at Washington Square Park, across the street from the Newberry. The two of them, on a bench, watching the world go by.

"Life is amazing," she said. "Chock-full of surprises."

He laughed. "Did I tell you I like your attitude?"

"Yeah. Once or twice…but I mean, really. Fifteen days ago, I was unemployed, worrying over where my next mortgage payment was going to come from. Tonight, I'm in San Francisco, watching the sea lions at Fisherman's Wharf after dinner at one of the best restaurants in California." *With you,* she silently added.

Tom was nodding. "Lucky you thought of giving TAKA-Hanson a try. And I mean lucky for both of us."

"Yeah. Lucky." Lucky her uncle Drake decided to give her a call....

Again, she considered just telling Tom about her uncle. But how far should she take it? Should she mention Drake's remarks about how he eventually wanted her to spy for him? And then fall all over herself promising Tom she'd never do such a thing?

No. Let it go.

Why take a chance of stirring up trouble for herself? She just wanted to do good work and enjoy the benefits of having a decent income and a job that had her jumping out of bed in the morning, eager to face the day. A job that included being with Tom…

In a strictly professional sense, of course.

"You okay?" He was looking at her sideways.

"Yeah. Great. Why?"

"I don't know. You looked a little grim there for a moment."

She smoothed her hair out of her face again. "No. Not grim. Not in the least."

He seemed to doubt her denial—but then he shrugged. "So. What was your take on Riki? You think he can get back on schedule?"

"Not my…er…field of expertise."

"I know. But just your gut feeling."

"I don't—"

"Winston. Stop hedging."

Winston. She liked it when he called her by her last name. Somehow, he made it seem so personal—his own private nickname for her. "Okay. My gut feeling…which is only that, a feeling…"

He made the move-it-along gesture.

"All right, all right. It's just...well, I know that things go wrong. It's the nature of any business. But gee. A whole lot is going wrong with Riki's end of things, don't you think?"

"You're suspicious."

"Well, yeah. A little."

"So am I. But it could be just a case of Murphy's Law on steroids. Stuff happens."

"But it's a *lot* of stuff."

"True. I'll go over all of it with Helen. Get her take on the situation. She should be meeting us in Kyoto...."

Helen. Shelly had heard a lot about Helen Taka-Hanson in her week and a half of working for Tom. The CEO of the hospitality division lived in Chicago with her husband, Morito Taka, who was usually called Mori and who was chairman of TAKA-Hanson's board. The couple had been in Japan since before Shelly got the job with Tom, so she had yet to meet either of them.

She watched a seagull as it strutted past on the wharf a few feet from the bench. "Riki did seem certain that he could pull it all into line."

"Doesn't mean he will."

"True. But he does have a good track record, right?"

"Right. And there is no way we're going to solve this problem tonight."

"True again."

"So. Want to take a cable car back to the hotel?"

"Does a sea lion poop in the bay?"

He rose. "I can't believe you said that."

"Tacky, huh?" She laughed.

He looked down at her. And she gazed up. It was one of those moments they write about in novels. Fireworks. Rockets. Shivers sliding down her spine. A few glorious seconds where the world faded away and there was only the two of them.

"Come on," he said softly. "Let's get moving."

Shelly slept with the curtains open that night, so that when she woke up in the morning, the first thing she saw was the fog shrouding the bay.

She and Tom shared a working breakfast in one of the hotel's restaurants. They went over her notes from the day before and he gave her instructions for working up a summary that he could pass on to Helen, to bring her up to speed for their meeting on the subject.

Their plane was supposed to take off at eleven-ten. But at one, they were still sitting in the airport waiting for some mechanical problem to be repaired.

Her cell rang. Tom shot her a questioning look. She glanced at the display. "My mom's number," she told him. "Which means it's probably Max." She hit Talk. "What's up?"

"Mom. My pollywog is growing two more legs."

"Wow. Not bad."

"They're kind of like stubs now, but they're getting bigger."

"You'll have a frog before you know it." Beside her, Tom chuckled. She sent him a grin, but he'd already gone back to reading e-mail. Max chattered away about swimming in the creek and getting up early to go fishing with his grandpa, about the chocolate cupcakes with white frosting that his granny made specially for him, about the two boys he'd met who were just his age.

When he paused for a breath, she asked, "So how are your glasses holding up?"

"Um. Well, Mom. We prob'ly need to talk about that."

"Can you still use them?"

"Yeah. Granny has lots of duct tape. But they're getting kind of crooked. They, um, fell off and I stepped on them. Grandpa bent them back so I can use them, and Granny put more tape on them, but they're not the same as they were before."

"Don't worry. I called and ordered you another pair. You think you can make them last until you get home?"

He said he could. Shelly talked to her mom.

When she said goodbye, Tom glanced up from his BlackBerry. "I had glasses when I was a kid. Couldn't see a damn thing without them. And I was always breaking them—or losing them."

"I've never seen you wear glasses."

"Laser surgery. Works wonders."

"Ah. Too bad they don't recommend it for children. I know it's not cheap, but it has to be better than buying a new pair of glasses every couple of months." He was looking at her strangely. "What?"

"You love being a mom, huh?"

"Yeah. Toughest job in the world. But somebody's got to do it."

"I always wanted kids…." He looked away.

"Tom?"

When he faced her, those fine blue eyes had real regret in them. "Never worked out. I've kind of kept on the move. Chasing the next promotion. The…timing was always off for starting a family."

She knew there was more to it. He'd told her Friday night that he'd had two serious relationships. What had happened with them? She wanted to know. A lot.

Too bad pushing him for his secrets wasn't an option—given she was doing her best to keep from getting too close to him and risking the possibility of her wonderful new job blowing up in her face.

"It's never too late," she said softly. "Especially for a guy. I mean, the, er, biological clock ticks on forever when you're a guy.…"

"Winston."

"What?"

"Are you trying to reassure me?"

"Well. Yeah."

"Thanks. I think." He spoke in a wry tone, but his eyes said he just might grab her and kiss her—a long, slow, deep, wet one. Right here in the airport, where everyone could see.

Would she mind that? Nope. Not in the least. She would just love that.

And there lay the problem.

She cleared her throat. "Uh. You're welcome—and they're calling our flight."

He was looking at her mouth. "They are?"

She laughed, and that broke the sensual spell that had somehow woven itself around them. "Let's go."

"Right." He looked away.

She felt…bereft. How dumb was that? She shook herself and shouldered her carry-on.

* * *

Wednesday, Shelly got into the office even earlier than usual. Since Tom would be gone Thursday and Friday, she had a lot of calls to field and appointments that still needed rescheduling. There were also her regular daily duties—filing, getting correspondence out and the like—that had to be finished for the week in that one day. Or at least, as close to finished as she could get them. She'd brought a sandwich so she could eat lunch at her desk. Every hour counted on a day like this one.

Lil strutted over at a little before noon. The sexy redhead sat on the edge of Shelly's desk and studied her manicure.

"You work too damn hard, Shel. You know that?"

Shelly kept on typing. "So much to do, so little time."

"Come with me. We'll go to O'Connell's." Lil named a local place where a lot of TAKA-Hanson's clerical staff hung out. "Get a beer and brats. Dish all the best dirt."

Shelly got to the end of a paragraph and leaned back in her chair. She indicated the brown bag with her sandwich in it. "Thanks. I'd love to. But it's not happening. Not today."

Lil rearranged the tape dispenser, moved the stapler an inch to the left. "San Francisco on Monday, Kyoto on Thursday. What a life, huh?"

Shelly laughed. "Lil, I swear. Is there anything that happens in this office you don't know about ahead of time?"

She put up both hands. "Okay, ya got me. I take a certain pride in being nosy as hell."

"Next week, maybe?"

"Well." Lil gave a lazy shrug. "We can hope, I guess. You're very dedicated. It's totally annoying." She sent Shelly a teasing smile to let her know she was joking, then tipped her head toward Tom's shut door. "So honestly, now. How's it going between you and the hunky CFO?"

"Great. Really."

"He likes you. I can tell." Was that jealousy Shelly spotted in those gorgeous green eyes? Or just another lead-in, an attempt to get Shelly to confide—so Lil could turn right around and blab every word she said?

Shelly played it straight. "I like him, too. Makes for an easier working relationship. It's all good."

"Oh, I'll bet."

Tom's line lit up. Shelly punched him in. "Yes?"

He asked, "What about the accounting review?"

"Moved it to next Tuesday, first of July."

"Okay. That'll work." His line went dark.

Lil eased her hip off the desk and straightened her tight skirt. "Well, all right. Be boring and work through lunch."

"Sorry. Next week?"

"Next week? Shel, anything could happen between now and then."

Something in her tone had Shelly shooting her a sharp glance. "Anything…like what?"

Lil waved a hand. "Oh, nothing. How about Monday?"

Shelly would have a full day Monday, too. But she didn't want to offend Lil. "Tuesday?"

"Why not?" Lil sauntered off toward the elevator. Shelly stared after her until she vanished from sight.

Already, Shelly was dreading next Tuesday's lunch. She wanted to stay on good terms with all of her coworkers, but spending time with Lil was exhausting. You had to be way careful not to say anything you didn't want the whole office to hear.

And was Lil after Tom? Last week in the break room, one of the other assistants had hinted that Lil had a thing going with her boss, Louie D'Amitri. Certainly a sexy, single CFO trumped a married, paunchy finance manager any day.

Shelly grinned to herself. Okay, she was feeling ridiculously smug. She just knew someone like Lil could never be Tom's type. Not that it mattered to Shelly, personally.

Or so she kept trying to convince herself—to little effect, unfortunately. She *did* care what kind of woman might interest her boss. She cared way too much.

Tom had hit the ground running, too, that day, and never stopped.

It was always crazy like this when he had two high-priority trips to deal with inside of one week. He had several meetings. Between those, he was briefing for the visit to the Kyoto site, catching up on voice mail and doing phone interviews with a couple of industry rags on the progress of TAKA-Hanson's new chain of luxury hotels.

Tom spun the interviews toward the exclusivity and originality of the new chain. He avoided pesky subjects such as Riki's failure to deliver on time and the cost overruns at the Kyoto site. The first interview, with *Service Providers Magazine* went off without hitch.

But then, later in the day, he talked to Chip Fast, from *Hotelier Monthly.* Tom liked Chip and Chip returned the sentiment, which was convenient for both of them. They always made a point to touch base, have dinner or at least a drink, whenever the reporter came to town. *Hotelier Monthly* had its offices in New York City.

After Tom gave Chip all the news that was fit to print, Chip had some inside information he didn't mind sharing with a friend. "Heard of the Thatcher Group?"

Tom got that sinking feeling low in his gut. "The name sounds familiar...." Too damn familiar.

"The Thatcher Group has an office here, in Manhattan. It's new. CEO and Chairman of the board is Drake Thatcher. You've probably heard of him. Been around forever. The stock market, banking, property development, you name it. The man's always got his fingers in the coming thing."

"I know of him." Tom made his voice offhand, though inside he was anything but.

"Well, now he's formed the Thatcher Group," said Chip.

"Hospitality?" Tom asked, as if he hadn't already figured it out.

"That's right. High-end hotels. International in scope. He'll be giving TAKA-Hanson a run for the money."

"You talked to Thatcher himself?"

"No. One of the partners." Chip gave a name and Tom made a note of it. "I didn't get much else. They're just in the planning stages. The guy I talked to said they were shooting for a San Francisco grand opening three years out—and then backpedaled like mad, said the location wasn't firmed up yet. Blah, blah, blah…"

San Francisco. Damn Thatcher's black soul to hell. "Competition," Tom said in a tone that gave away none of his fury. "Always good for business."

"Just thought you'd like to know."

"Thanks, Chip."

"I'll give you a call when I hear more…."

"And be sure to let me know next time you're in town. We'll get together."

"Right back at ya."

Tom hung up. He buzzed Shelly. "Hold my calls."

"Will do," she answered brightly, just the sound of her voice cheering him up.

The buoyant feeling didn't last. His former mentor and long-time nemesis had surfaced once again. The man who set Tom up to go to jail, the man who tried to destroy Tom over and over.

Drake in the hotel business…

Tom's stomach twisted. How long would it be before Thatcher made his move to push Tom out of the picture? Tom didn't get it. Never had. After all, *he'd* paid the price fourteen years ago while Drake got away clean. But for some reason, Thatcher seemed driven to mess Tom over every chance he got. As if Drake had been the one to end up royally screwed all those years ago.

In Dallas that last time, Tom had learned, well after the fact, that Drake had called Tom's boss to discredit him.

Tom had lost that job. He'd gone too long without finding another one. At the time, he'd been in a relationship. A serious one. The relationship hadn't survived the stress of his long-term unemployment. Neither had the baby his fiancée was carrying.

That was the worst of all the damages Drake Thatcher had inflicted on him: the loss of an innocent unborn child.

Not that Drake had stopped there. In New York a few years ago Thatcher had had a long conversation with someone on the board of Tom's company. Tom hadn't been fired either time. He'd been called in and told it was best if he moved on. No one wanted trouble. Tom certainly didn't. He'd had trouble enough already in his life.

He was given good severance packages and glowing recommendations. Since he'd suspected both times that Drake was the reason he was out of a job, he called in markers, did his research—and had his suspicions confirmed.

The second time, in New York three years ago, he'd tracked Thatcher down and confronted him. Drake denied everything.

Tom had seriously considered murder then. Or, at least, finding a way to cause Thatcher's destruction, however he could manage that.

He still didn't really know why he'd walked away from the tempting prospect of revenge.

But he had. He'd walked away and made *another* new life for himself with TAKA-Hanson.

At least this time, since Tom had been truthful with Helen from the start, Drake wouldn't be able to cost him his job just by filling Helen in on Tom's shady past.

Thatcher in the hospitality business…

It couldn't be good. Drake always kept a close eye on the competition. Too close. Did he already have spies infiltrating TAKA-Hanson?

Suddenly, Tom saw the issues with the interiors in San Francisco, and the problems in Kyoto in a whole new light. Could Drake be behind it all?

Tom grunted. No need to get paranoid. Drake Thatcher meant trouble, yeah. But cost overruns and designers running behind schedule… Things like that were bound to happen.

Then again, the situation with Riki seemed especially extreme. Could that much be going wrong with flooring and furnishings, all at once, without a little help?

They could and he knew it. It was the nature of the beast. It was business. Things went wrong and you dealt with them. There was little to be gained by manufacturing conspiracy theories.

He considered calling Helen right then. But it was barely 5:00 a.m. in Tokyo—and this unpleasant news was nothing that couldn't wait until he saw her Friday, when she met him in Kyoto. He would prefer to discuss it face-to-face, anyway.

Yeah.

It could wait. This was hardly a crisis.

It was more like a warning sign.

Tom knew Drake Thatcher. Whatever project Drake took on, he had to be the best at it. The man would stoop pretty damn low to deal a blow to any competitor.

And wait…

Tom was getting ahead of himself. It was always

possible that Chip had bad intel on this. The reporter had said he'd talked to one of Thatcher's partners, but he hadn't mentioned whether he'd checked around to confirm the reliability of the source.

Tom picked up the phone and made some calls. He had sources of his own, after all.

An hour later, he was certain.

Drake Thatcher had moved over into the hotel business. TAKA-Hanson would need to be ready to deal with Drake's dirty tricks.

Chapter Four

Early Thursday morning, Tom and Shelly took one of the TAKA-Hanson jets to Kyoto. With the hour-long layover for refueling in San Francisco, the trip took fourteen hours.

Shelly worked through some of the flight and napped the rest. Tom had suggested the nap. He planned that they'd go right to work as soon as they landed. A little sleep on the plane would keep jet lag from slowing them down too much.

When they touched down at the private airstrip in Kyoto, it was a little after nine Thursday night, Chicago time. In Japan, it was lunchtime on Friday.

It was also raining—torrential rain. Walls of water poured out of the sky. The pretty Asian woman who'd taken care of them through the flight provided rain slickers.

"Welcome to Kyoto," she said. "As it happens, you visit our beautiful city in the season of monsoons."

Shelly took the yellow slicker—and used the opportunity to practice her rudimentary Japanese. "*Dōmo arigatō.*" Thank you very much.

The pretty woman bowed. "*Dō itashi mashite.*" You're welcome.

"Let's go." Tom already had his slicker on. Shelly donned hers and they raced for the limo that waited for them on the tarmac.

Once they were safe in the comfort of the big car, with their bags safely stowed in the trunk, Tom told the driver to take them to the construction site.

Shelly would have admired the scenery—if it had been more than a blur through all that water. On the other side of the car, Tom sat, silent. He seemed preoccupied, as he had through most of the flight.

She wanted to reach across, touch his hand. Ask him if he was all right. But since she was trying to keep things professional, she hesitated to give him any contradictory signals.

He must have felt her worried gaze on him. "What?" His nose was shiny with rain and water glistened in his dark brows, stuck his eyelashes together.

She flipped back the hood of her slicker and brushed at her cheeks with both hands. "I'm soaked. Slicker or not."

"And you will be wetter, believe me."

She couldn't wait to get to the hotel where they were

staying, to take a long bath and indulge in a good night's sleep. But work came first. Now, they were headed for The Taka Kyoto. Tom got out his BlackBerry and called the site, told them to except his arrival within the hour.

After that, they were quiet. There was the rain drumming on the roof and the low drone of the driver's radio.

When they arrived at the site, Shelly saw mud—a lot of it—and rain-soaked concrete. She spotted two enormous building cranes, one at either end of the site. The Taka Kyoto rose from the rubble of ongoing construction. Through the veil of the rain, the building itself appeared more or less complete.

"It looks as far along as the San Francisco hotel," she said to Tom.

He sent her a grim glance. "Trust me. It's not. We got the whole thing closed up before the rains started. But inside, we've got a long way to go and less than six months to do it in."

The driver steered the limo to a row of trailers. They flipped their yellow hoods back over their heads, grabbed their briefcases and made a run for it. Tom raced for the nearest, biggest trailer, Shelly right behind him.

A middle-aged Asian woman pushed the door open for them. They ran in. "You made it." She smiled. Her accent was as American as a big slice of homemade apple pie.

"Thanks, Akiko." Tom was already shrugging out of the dripping slicker. Shelly followed suit. Tom said, "Akiko is Robby's assistant."

"Hey," said Akiko, turning her bright smile on Shelly. A man in shirtsleeves came through a door a few feet away. Brown hair, white shirt, tan slacks. Maybe five-ten. He was ordinary to the point of blandness, the kind of guy you would pass on the street and never give a second glance.

Tom said, "Shelly, this is Robby Axelrod."

Robby nodded. "Great to meet you, Shelly." He rubbed his hands together. "Well, Tom. How 'bout lunch?"

"Can you have something brought in?"

"Of course." Robby glanced at Akiko, who gave him a nod. "Right away," she said.

"And coffee," added Robby.

"Will do," said Akiko.

The construction manager led the way through the open door to the main area of the long trailer, which was an on-site conference room. Ned Jones, the new accountant on the site, stood from the table and Robby introduced him. Ned had been hired just recently, when the original accountant was forced to return to the States.

"Family issues," Robby explained, shaking his head.

The afternoon progressed pretty much like the day with the designer in San Francisco. Robby had valid reasons for all the ways construction was running behind schedule. The rains, he said, caused no end of delays. Trucks carrying equipment and material didn't arrive on time—if they arrived at all. That meant the subcontractors lined up to do the job had to move on to something else. And then, when the material did arrive, Robby had to get another sub or wait for the first one to become available again.

Yes, there'd been some accounting issues—subs being paid before the work was done, material paid for that hadn't been delivered yet. There were requisitions stuck in processing, so that material and equipment were never ordered in the first place. But all that, Robby and Ned explained, had occurred because the previous accountant had been distracted by the long illness of his wife back home.

Ned, Robby insisted, was on top of the problem. He was switching them over to a whole new payables/receivables system. Robby was pleased with the way he was cleaning up the accounting end.

Tom shook his head. "I've seen the reports. Sorry, Ned. But most of the problems have occurred since you took over."

Ned, who was tall, blond and square-jawed, explained, "To start, I tried working within my predecessor's system. I never like to come on a job and make changes right off the bat. I like to see what works and what doesn't, and then proceed from there. We're just moving on to using my system now."

"And we need to give the new system a chance to work," Robby argued.

Tom looked from one man to the other. "Of course, we'll give it a chance. How long till it's up to speed?"

"We're getting there," said Robby, with a nervous glance at Ned.

Tom pressed for a commitment. "You're telling me the accounting issues are a thing of the past as of this moment?"

Robby hedged. "Any system takes tweaking. You'll need to give us a few weeks to work out the kinks."

"We don't have a few weeks."

"I know. And I didn't mean to put up a red flag here. You'll be seeing improvement immediately. Right, Ned?"

"That's right." Ned was all square-jawed firmness and determination. "Now we just need to finish cleaning up the mess."

Tom nodded. "Good. I'll be watching the numbers. Closely."

"And you'll like what you see," Ned promised.

The rain had slowed to a drizzle by the time the limo dropped Shelly and Tom off at their hotel.

"Take the evening for yourself," he said, when they reached her room.

"You don't need me for dinner with Robby and Ned?"

"Order room service," he said. "Rest up. Be fresh for tomorrow, when the meetings will be endless and we'll also have the thrills and chills of touring the site."

"Ugh. Even if the rain stops, it's going to be muddy."

"True. But at least Akiko has a cabinet full of rubber boots. In a range of sizes."

"Good news. I guess I won't have to sacrifice a pair of shoes, after all."

She should say good-night. But she didn't. She felt reluctant to leave him. After the long flight, when he'd been wrapped up in his own concerns, and the endless tension-filled meeting over the problems at the site, it was nice to share a quiet minute, just the two of them.

And he didn't seem any more eager to leave her than she was to see him go. So why not? A little small talk. What could it hurt?

"I feel guilty," she confessed. "Leaving you on your own."

"Hey. I'll have Robby and Ned."

"True...." He had a tiny scar over his left eye, a thin, pale line, long-healed. How had that happened?

He laughed. "What?"

"Nothing. Really— So. Room service. A good night's sleep. What's not to like? And you get the guys' night out." Three harried-looking businessman-types came striding toward them. Shelly tugged on the retractable handle of her suitcase and backed to the wall beside the door to her room, out of their way.

Tom moved in closer as the strangers rushed by. "Tomorrow night's another story." He smelled of the rain and that subtle aftershave he wore. And his face was shadowed with a day's growth of dark beard. She wanted to reach up and touch his rough cheek, to let her hand trail down until she clasped his big shoulder. She could just feel the hardness of his muscles beneath the fine fabric of his jacket....

She kept her hands to herself and remembered it was her turn to talk. "What's happening tomorrow night?"

"You'll be working." His voice was low, almost intimate. The sound of it warmed her. "Helen and Mori will be here. We'll have dinner with them, just the four of us."

"That's great. I can't wait to meet the fabulous Helen and her Samurai tycoon husband."

Tom braced a hand on the wall near her head. "Who told you Mori Taka was a Samurai tycoon?"

"That's what Verna always called him. The Samurai Tycoon—usually followed by a sigh. She said he has dark, piercing eyes and a commanding presence. I think she kind of had a crush on him."

Tom grunted. "Come on. Verna?"

Shelly laughed. "Just a fantasy crush."

"Verna's married."

"Fantasy, Tom. As in, not in the real world."

"She's a *grandmother.*"

"So? Grandmothers have fantasy lives too, you know."

"I never said they didn't."

"Tom. Come on. You said 'Verna's a grandmother,' *implying* that you believe grandmothers don't have fantasy lives."

"I implied no such thing. *Helen's* a grandmother. I don't know about her fantasy life, but I have no trouble believing she has one."

"But Helen's hot, right?"

"And by that you mean…?"

"Helen may be a grandmother, but she's not grand-mother*ly.* You seem to think that grandmotherly women don't have fantasy lives. I'm here to tell you, they do. Or at least, Verna does."

He shook his head. Slowly. "You should have been a lawyer." A smile flirted with the corners of his sexy mouth. "You'd have killed 'em in every cross." He moved in an inch closer, bringing with him that clean scent of rain and the warmth of his big body.

"I never wanted to be a lawyer," she said and wished her voice hadn't suddenly gone husky.

"No? Then what?"

"I planned to study finance. You're lucky Max came along. I'd be competing for your job."

"I think you'd be damn good at whatever you decided to do."

"Why, thank you…."

"You could still go back to school, you know." He touched her face. And she let him. So lightly, he traced the fall of her hair where it lay along her cheek, curling slightly from the rain. She reveled in that touch—at the same time as she reminded herself that it didn't mean anything.

That it was innocent.

Innocent. Right. She knew it was anything but.

And what were they talking about? Oh. Her going back to college. "It's possible," she said, the huskiness more pronounced than before. "In the future. Right now, though, I've got this demanding job. Takes up most of my time. Lucky I happen to love it, huh?"

"Lucky. Oh, yeah…"

She tried valiantly to remember all the reasons she could never do something so foolish and unprofessional as kiss him. But the whole world was there in those summer-sky eyes of his. And along her cheek, she could still feel the memory of his touch—an echo of sensation, so sweet. So…right.

And his lips… What red-blooded woman wouldn't want a kiss from those lips of his?

She whispered, "Tom, we shouldn't be doing this."

"What?"

"As if you didn't know."

"I don't. I'm innocent. I haven't got a clue what you're talking about."

"Oh, please. You know. Standing here in this hallway,

together, behaving in a manner that's a long way from professional."

"It's just small talk. Nothing wrong with that."

"It's more than small talk. You know it is."

"You think?"

"I know." And she made it worse. She gave in to her desire to reach up, to lay her hand along the side of his beard-scratchy cheek.

He whispered her name as his mouth met hers.

So lightly, he kissed her. A hello kind of a kiss, a let-me-taste-you kiss, a butterfly brushing of his lips on hers.

No, she thought. *Shouldn't be doing this. Bad, bad move…*

And simultaneously, a joyous voice in her head shouted, *Yes! Yes, yes, yes, yes…*

When he pulled back to look at her, she still had her palm pressed against his cheek. She gulped and broke the contact.

His mouth remained two inches from hers and his eyes…oh, his eyes… "I shouldn't have done that, huh?"

She let out a slow sigh. "Oh, probably not."

"We'll just pretend it never happened."

This was very serious and she knew she shouldn't laugh. Still, a low giggle escaped. "Pretend it didn't happen. Wish me luck with that."

"I'm lying," he said. "I won't pretend anything of the kind."

"Yeah. Well. I would. If I could."

"But you can't." The blue eyes gleamed, the summer-sky sweetness fled. Now the blue was dangerous, wild and full of mystery as the deep blue sea. He wanted her.

As she wanted him.

She whispered, "A week ago, that bench at Washington Square Park, in front of the Newberry…"

He remembered. "You told me this wasn't going to happen."

"And look at us now."

"Shelly. It was just a kiss."

"Yeah. Right. How many times did you kiss Verna?"

"Don't get on me again about Verna. I was wrong and I'm willing to admit it. A grandmother has a right to her fantasies, just like the rest of us."

"I wasn't referring to Verna's fantasies. You're deliberately misunderstanding me."

"What? Me?"

"I repeat, how many times did you kiss Verna?"

"I kissed her last Friday night, as a matter of fact."

"Cheater. On the cheek, you kissed her."

"A kiss is a kiss."

She groaned. "Liar, liar, pants on fire…"

He leaned closer still, so his rough cheek brushed her soft one. A sweet shiver ran through her as he whispered in her ear. "You feel it, like I do. It's…special. Between you and me."

She put her hands on his hard, warm chest and pushed gently—until he backed away enough that she could look him in the eye. "Office romances are a bad idea. They never—"

"Stop." He put his index finger against her lips.

"But I—"

"Shh. Listen. Are you listening?"

She made a face at him. "Hit me with it."

"I have examples."

"Of?"

"Offices romances that worked out great. Better than great."

"Oh, yeah, right, sure."

"Let's see…. Jack Hanson, Helen's stepson, and his wife, Samantha. Samantha and Jack were old business rivals. Then she came to work at Hanson Media—with Jack. And then there's David Hanson, George Hanson's brother. He actually married his secretary, Nina. Can you believe that?"

"Okay, okay. I'll modify my position."

"You bet you will."

"*Sometimes* office romances do work out."

"Say that again."

"I'm willing to admit that not all office romances end badly. How's that?"

"Better."

She cleared her throat. Still, when she spoke her voice came out breathless and much too hopeful. "So. Are you going to…kiss me again?"

"I should." He dropped his hand from the wall beside her and stepped back. "But breathe easy. You're safe from my kisses. For the moment, anyway."

"You've got to stop making me want to believe you," she told him, softly—and much too sincerely. "You know that, don't you?"

"There's no damn harm in believing the truth." He sighed. "See you at breakfast tomorrow. At 7:00 a.m."

"I'll be ready."

He left her, wheeling his suitcase to the next door down and disappearing inside.

Chapter Five

Tom was waiting in the booth when Shelly entered the hotel coffee shop the next morning. The hostess brought her to him.

She wore a straight skirt and a snug white shirt and he thought he'd never seen a woman so fresh and sweet and sexy, all at the same time. Shamelessly enjoying the view, he watched her slide into the seat opposite him.

"Coffee," she said to the hostess. "Thanks...." She gave the other woman that amazing wide smile. And then she turned to him. He watched the color bloom upward over he neck and cheeks. "Tom. You're staring."

"Yeah. I am. Is that a problem for you?"

"I don't think I'm going to answer that question." She glanced at her watch. "It's six-thirty."

"So?"

"You're way early, Tom."

"You, too."

"But I'm always early. It's my job to be here ahead of you."

"I was up. I came on down."

"You look tired."

"I am, a little. The dinner with Robby and Ned went late. And the problems at the site…"

"You're worried."

"Let's just say I'm concerned." And making matters worse was the specter of Drake Thatcher. Tom looked into those understanding brown eyes across the booth from him and again found himself considering telling her.

All of it. From his early ruthless ambition that had him attaching himself to a high-end crook like Thatcher, through his disgrace and imprisonment, on to the other jobs he'd lost because of Thatcher's intervention—and what losing those jobs had cost him. Then she would understand the stakes when he said he'd learned that Thatcher was now setting himself up in the hospitality business.

But no. It wasn't her problem. On a need-to-know basis, she didn't.

Maybe someday, if things progressed between them in the way he couldn't help but hope they might. Maybe then.

Right now, though, they had a long day ahead of them. They needed to focus on that.

Her coffee came and she ordered eggs. When the

waitress left them, she asked, "So how did the dinner go last night?"

"It was fine. We went to this steakhouse Robby likes in Osaka. Ned did most of the talking, which was good. I got to know him a little. I have high hopes he'll work out better than the last guy."

They discussed the schedule for the day: a tour of the site, another meeting with Robby and the accountant. Helen would be arriving around noon. He needed a private meeting with her.

"We'll leave the afternoon open," he said. "See how the day shapes up. And then dinner."

"I really am looking forward to that." She sipped her coffee. "I mean, it's all fascinating, being here in Japan, learning how things work on a big construction site. But dinner with the CEO and the Chairman of the Board. What's not to like about that?"

The tour of the site just made Tom more aware of all that wasn't getting done.

Helen arrived at the office trailers at eleven-thirty. Mori, she said, was held up in Tokyo, but he would join them in the evening. Tom introduced her to Shelly.

Akiko went out and got deli sandwiches for everyone. Tom and Helen took theirs to one of the other trailers, where they could speak privately.

He filled her in on the details of the problems in San Francisco first. "So I gave Riki the space to turn things around," he concluded. "But in the meantime, I think we should be looking for someone to pick up the pieces and pull it together if he doesn't get it under control."

Helen nodded. "I'll put the word out. How about the issues here?"

"Again, I think we have to give Robby and Ned a chance. Things have been pretty much on schedule here until the past month. They assure me they can catch up."

Helen agreed. It wasn't time to pull the plug on anyone. Yet.

"And there's something else…" *Thatcher*. He hardly knew how to begin on that one.

Helen sipped the tea she'd ordered with her sandwich. "The look on your face is not reassuring."

"Bear with me here."

"Of course."

"Two years ago, when I told you I'd been convicted of insider trading…"

"Yes?"

"I didn't go into the details. It didn't seem necessary then. But my immediate supervisor at the time I was fired was a man named Drake Thatcher. I was a greedy kid, in a hurry to make it big, willing to do whatever I had to to get ahead. Thatcher took my ambition and used it for his own purposes. He passed me the tips that got me six months in prison, and told me who to give them to. I got caught. He didn't."

Helen's smile was rueful. "I have excellent investigators, Tom. They reported that Drake Thatcher had been your boss on Wall Street. I had them look into his background a little. As I remember, he's from an important family. But some of his dealings haven't been exactly aboveboard…"

"…And you're wondering why I decided to lay all this on you now?"

She shrugged. "I'm sure you're getting to it."

"I just want you to know that I've had other run-ins with Thatcher. I never ended up in jail again, so that's something, I guess. But because of him and his interference, I've lost more than one job."

Much worse than the jobs, he'd lost two parents, a couple of serious relationships. And perhaps worst of all, one innocent unborn child. None of which he intended to mention to his CEO. He admired and respected Helen. He even considered her a friend. But this was business. Here, his personal losses didn't apply, even as deep as they cut him, which was clear to the bone.

Tom continued, "You could say I'm unreasonably suspicious of Drake, and you might be right. So what I'm telling you should be taken with a grain of salt. Or two. Anything I say about Drake Thatcher is going to be colored by the fact that I despise the man. Still, I thought you should know this. A heads-up never hurts."

"I understand. What's going on?"

He told her what Chip Fast had told him.

When he finished, she asked, "You've double-checked this story?"

"I have. Drake Thatcher's in the hotel business, all right. And given what I know about the man, I would bet my last year's production bonus that we're in for trouble."

In her hotel room at seven-fifteen that evening, Shelly dabbed on a little perfume and stood back to give herself a final look in the mirror. She smoothed her hair and turned to glance over her shoulder at the view from the rear.

Was she nervous? Well, a little. And excited, too. A night out in Kyoto, with Tom. She kept reminding herself that it was a business dinner. Still, somehow, it felt like a date.

Most of the day she'd kept her mind firmly on doing her job, which meant she didn't allow herself to get lost in daydreams of the amazing, sexy, intriguing man who happened to be her boss. By keeping things strictly business, even in her thoughts, she'd managed *not* to dwell on those few moments in the hallway last night, managed not to fade off into self-indulgent fantasies— of the feel of his lips brushing hers, of the promise in his blue eyes, of the real tenderness in his voice when he pressed her to admit that not all office romances end in disaster.

But now it was evening, with their almost-date ahead of her, now she was checking herself out in the mirror, wanting to be sure she looked her best for him…

Now, she let the sensual thoughts flood over her. They stirred her blood, made her feel hot and yearning beneath her skin. She'd known him for two weeks and already she couldn't imagine *not* knowing him.

As if, in some strange way, he'd always been there, in her life. Just waiting for her to find him.

Her sleeveless dress was one of those traveler knits that didn't wrinkle. Still, she smoothed the front of it and lifted a hand to her hair. As each day went by, she was having more and more trouble remembering how important it was to keep things strictly professional with Tom.

She found herself wondering, why *couldn't* it work out between them? Why did she necessarily have to jump ahead to the prospect of heartbreak? Why *not* take a chance?

Because I can't afford to lose this job, that's why.

Then again, wouldn't there always be some reason or other to say no to passion, to love, to the hope of a lifetime with a good man at her side?

There was a tap on the door. *Tom.* Her heart beat a happy tattoo under her breastbone. Sheesh. She was grinning like a fool, just at the sound of his knock. Grabbing her satin clutch from the bathroom counter, she went to answer.

Something happened, there at the door. Maybe it was the welcoming, eager smile she gave him. Maybe it was her desire for him shining in her eyes.

Whatever.

He must have seen her willingness. He took a step forward, into the room. She moved back. The door swung shut, closing them in together.

And Shelly decided. Just like that, as the latch clicked with a small, but final, sound.

She was through running away from this—from Tom, from all the rich and sweet possibilities she sensed might be theirs, from the promise she saw in his eyes. She was taking a chance on him…on *them*.

Starting right now.

"You look good," he said.

"Thank you." Slowly, with purpose, she laid her hand

against his warm, hard chest. She felt…liberated. Freed at last from the strict constraints of her role as his assistant.

She wanted more from him. So very much more.

His gaze locked on her trembling mouth. "You smell good, too." He reached for her. She melted closer. "Better than good…" He lowered his mouth to hers.

She dropped her clutch to the carpet and kissed him back. Heaven was in that kiss. It felt so fine, his warm, hard body touching hers, his strong arms around her. She lifted her other hand and rested it, too, on the expensive silk of his jacket. His chest was broad and strong, just right for a woman to lean on. She sighed as he deepened the kiss. She dared to grasp his big shoulders, to pull him even closer.

Closer.

Yes.

Closer…

Eventually, he lifted his head and gazed down at her. "Well."

"Well, what?" She straightened his power tie.

"What a great way to start an evening."

"Let me make myself perfectly clear," she whispered.

"By all means," he replied.

"It's like this…." And she went on tiptoe to capture those lips of his all over again.

Oh, yes! Kissing him was everything kissing a man ought to be. She loved the way his mouth fitted hers, the tempting pressure as he urged her to greater intimacy. A secret sigh escaped her as she opened for him, as she welcomed the sweet invasion of his tongue.

Oh, yes. There was no other word for it. *Yes...*

After an endless time that was over much too soon, he raised his head again. "I could stand here forever, with you in my arms."

She made a low, rueful sound. "But Helen and her husband wouldn't understand."

His mouth was softer, redder, from kissing her. "Later," he promised. "All night."

She said the only word that mattered. "Yes."

Shelly thought Mori Taka was every bit as intense and attractive as Verna had claimed he would be. And Helen, who wore sleek red silk, seemed even more stunningly beautiful by candlelight than she had in her designer business clothes that afternoon. She and Mori were clearly very much in love. Though Mori had about him an air of quiet reserve, in keeping with his culture, the way he looked at Helen left no doubt that there was only one woman in the world for him.

At the construction site that afternoon, Helen had been kind and welcoming to Shelly, asking her how she was settling in at TAKA-Hanson. Now, she was curious about Shelly, the person.

Shelly told her about Max, and then about her mom and dad. "Married since time began. Still going strong..."

"Family." Mori gave a regal nod. "Nothing matters more."

Helen spoke freely of her own grown stepchildren. Jack, Andrew and Evan, George Hanson's sons, worked in the media and technology arms of the company stateside. All three were happily married.

Shelly slid Tom a glance when Helen mentioned Jack. She could see in his eyes that he remembered last night, when he'd used Jack and his wife, Samantha, as examples of office romances with happy endings.

"I also have a daughter, Jenny," said Helen. "She's married, too. Her husband, Richard Warren, is my long-time attorney."

Mori laid his lean, dark hand over his wife's alabaster one. "Only Kimiko remains single. She is, as you Americans would say, a handful."

Helen sent him a gently chiding look. "Kimi is a true original."

"Perhaps *too* original," said Mori in a dry tone. "I often think I should have arranged a marriage for her long ago, found her a strong-minded husband to take her in hand."

Helen laughed. "As if you would ever do such a thing to Kimi—not to mention the fact that she'd never stand for it." She sent her husband a fond look before explaining to Shelly, "Kimi's twenty-one, in summer school at the University of Pennsylvania now. Though she was born and raised mostly here in Japan, she's always loved all things American. I can't help but think of her as my own. But her mom was Mori's first wife."

The talk shifted from family to business. They briefly discussed future hotel sites. And Mori mentioned some of the new developments in the technology arm of the company.

Too soon, it was time for dessert. Shelly had *ichigo daifuku,* a round cake, iced and filled with a sweet red bean paste called *anko.* In the heart of the cake, wrapped in *anko,* was a plump red strawberry.

It was almost eleven when they got up to leave the restaurant. Helen said how pleased she was to have had a little time to get to know Shelly. "Tom…" She tipped her blond head to the side. "A moment?" She and Tom took the lead.

Shelly walked out with Mori, and got a little more practice on her rudimentary Japanese. She told him how much she'd appreciated the evening and he replied graciously that he'd enjoyed meeting her.

The way Tom glanced back at Shelly as he and Helen led the way through the glass doors, she had a feeling the CEO had just said something about her. A pair of limousines waited at the curb, one for Helen and Mori, a second for Shelly and Tom.

Inside the second limo, as the car wove through nighttime traffic, Tom confirmed Shelly's suspicions about what Helen had told him. "Helen says you're a winner." He reached across the seat and ran the back of his finger along her bare arm. The touch was electric. It stole her breath. "She says if I've got half the sense I need to be her CFO, I'll never let you get away."

Shelly warmed at such praise. She teased, "Did you tell her I was going somewhere?"

"Hell, no. I told her not to worry. I fully realize what an amazing woman you are and I plan to keep you good and close—and I don't just mean professionally."

His words thrilled her. "I'm glad," she told him softly, her gaze on the road ahead.

"Me, too."

She rested her hand on the seat between them. As she'd hoped he might, he laid his over it. Incredible, how just the feel of his hand on hers sent all her nerves singing a bold, happy song.

After a moment or two, she turned her hand over, palm up, so they could twine their fingers together.

"This could be interesting," she said as the lights of Kyoto glittered ahead of them and flew past on either side.

"Better than interesting." His tone was gruff.

She turned her head and sought his gaze through the shadows of the dark car. "You think so?"

He caught her glance and held it. "I know so."

Chapter Six

In the bedroom of Tom's suite, the blankets were already drawn back on the wide bed. The sheets had a blue-white luster in the darkness.

Shelly's heart beat hard and deep as he turned a lamp on low. In its golden glow, the white sheets warmed to the color of cream.

It all seemed…unreal, suddenly. Magical. A dream come true. And scary, too.

Was she really about to take this huge step with him? She knew all the reasons she shouldn't be doing this, yet here she was anyway.

Was she making a terrible, irrevocable mistake?

"Hey." He touched her shoulders, his hands so warm and firm. Strong. He seemed to her the kind of man she could lean on, the kind of man she could trust. Oh, God. She prayed that she was right. "Hey…"

She made herself tip her chin high and meet those eyes that had entranced her from that first moment they'd met, when Verna had pushed open the door to his office and she had stepped inside.

Had she known then that it would come to this? Life was so strange, really.

You went along, day-to-day, making do, making ends meet. Yes, there was joy. Fulfillment even—at doing good work. At watching your child grow from a helpless bundle in your arms to a kid with a great vocabulary and a passion for frogs and vanilla ice cream…

It all seemed enough. A good life, a rich one in the ways that really mattered, though money was tight.

So you went out, took a chance, got yourself something better.

And then, suddenly…

This: a certain look, a tone of voice, the touch of a certain hand.

And everything changed. All at once there was such wonder, such mystery. All at once, there was desire. Excitement. A dream of a future with this one special man.

"Hey," he said again.

And she reached up and touched his face, because at last she could. At last, they had come to this, to the two of them in a darkened room, alone. She ran her fingers up into his thick, dark hair. It felt so silky, so warm and alive.

He caught her wrist. She folded her fingers around his hand and he kissed her knuckles, one by one. "That first day, when Verna sent you in to me…"

A happy laugh escaped her. "I was just thinking of the first day, too."

"I thought you were exactly what I was looking for. I was so right."

"I thought you were a hunk."

"No kidding?" One side of his sinfully sexy mouth quirked up.

"Oh, yeah. I wondered whether it would be a problem, having a hot guy for a boss. I decided your hotness wouldn't be an issue. That I wouldn't *let* it be. So much for what I decided, huh?" She pulled on his hand and they went, together, to the terrace window.

Between the wide-open curtains, they saw the lights of Kyoto spreading into the distance, the faint dark shapes of rounded mountains beyond. "It's beautiful," she whispered.

"*You're* beautiful." He turned her to face him.

She found it difficult, all at once, to meet his eyes. So she focused on the top two buttons of his shirt. They were undone. He'd already taken off his jacket and his tie. The section of skin revealed between the open buttons was bronze-colored, tempting her.

She couldn't resist. She leaned into him, pressed her lips to that warm flesh between the open sides of his shirt. His skin felt so smooth beneath her kiss. She breathed in, slow and deep, scenting him.

He wrapped his big arms around her, and held her close. She reveled in the sweet pressure of his lips in her hair, in the heat and hardness of his body, touching all along the length of hers. He tipped up her chin with a finger and covered her mouth with his in a kiss that was slow and lazy. And so deep.

His warm fingers glided downward, skimming her hips. He gathered the skirt of her dress in his fists and slowly dragged it upward. Over her thighs, her hips, her panties, the curve of her waist.

She sighed when he broke the kiss to pull the dress the rest of the way over her head.

On the soft, cream-colored sheets, they lay together, naked. He caressed her, those tender hands of his learning her body, touching her in ways that aroused and excited her.

She reveled in each separate caress. He cupped her breasts in both of his hands and he kissed them, lavishing attention on one and then the other. He trailed kisses upward, along her neck, over her chin, until he found her mouth again and claimed it in another deep, searing kiss.

She whispered, "I love your kisses." Which only encouraged him to kiss her some more.

His hardness pressed against her hip and she eased her hand between them, to take him in her palm, to wrap her hungry fingers around him, to run her thumb over the silky head, until he moved in a rhythm like waves and groaned into her mouth. His breath was her breath, it was all one. She rolled to face him, so that he rubbed against her core, his body making promises.

The kind he would be keeping.

Soon.

Oh, yes. So soon…

His hand found her. With sure, knowing fingers, he parted her. She helped him, spreading her legs for him, still holding on to him, stroking him so that as he caressed her, he moaned at what she was doing to him.

What he did to her thrilled her, made her weak and limp with pleasure. He took her over. Took control. So she let him go with a moan, used her hands instead to clutch the sheets.

Whatever he wanted. She was open to him. She was his in that moment, as she'd never been anyone's. Ever. Not in her whole life long…

She tossed her head on the pillow as he touched her, as he moved down her body and captured her with his mouth, hooking one strong leg over her thigh, and then the other, sliding between her open legs to kiss her in the deepest, most intimate way.

She reached for him, spearing her fingers into his hair, holding him there, against her, so tight, so right, as he continued to kiss her, to suck on the small bud of flesh that was her most sensitive spot.

It didn't take long.

A few minutes of such concentrated attention and pleasure cascaded through her in waves, waves that centered down to the core of her, where he pleasured her so skillfully. The pleasure drew down, tight and shining—and then broke. Ripples of sensation claimed her whole body.

She cried out his name at the finish—only to discover it wasn't the finish at all. Her body humming in afterglow, she watched him through lazy-lidded eyes as he reached for the condom he'd left on the bedside table.

He sheathed himself and she felt arousal bloom again within her, warm and dark and oh, so sweet. She sighed in newly stirred longing and reached out her arms to him.

He held back. "Do you believe this is happening?"

She knew exactly how he felt. "It's like a dream, huh?"

"I hope I never wake up."

"Come here. Please. Here to me…"

He came down to her, bracing himself between her open thighs. His eyes were dark as agates then. The finely cut muscles of his chest and arms bulged as he held his weight above her. A fine sheen of sweat beaded his brow. She traced the sleek line of hair that tracked the center of his torso, all the way down…

Until she found him, grasped him, guided him into her.

Smooth. So smooth and easy. He filled her up and her body gave way to him, wanting him, needing him. She was ready.

So ready. She wrapped herself so tightly around him, taking him deep.

And he swept her away again, going with her that time. She let the rhythm carry her, she abandoned herself to sensation. He pushed in so deep and she took him hungrily.

As she felt her body gather for another shuddering release, he pushed up on his hands again and reared up above her.

"Shelly…" It was a rough whisper, an intimate call.

She opened her eyes and looked at him. "Yes," she answered. "Oh, yes…"

And then the pleasure claimed her again. She tossed her head on the pillows, reaching, grabbing his hard shoulders and pulling him down close to her again, so his sculpted chest crushed her breasts and she could take his mouth in a hungry kiss.

The finish washed over them, sweet as a honeycomb, intoxicating as the finest wine.

Tom propped himself up on an elbow and gazed down at Shelly. Damn, she was beautiful. Her skin had a glow and her brown hair was so pretty, spread out in shining tangles on the pillow.

"What?" She touched his face, her fingers soft and cool against his cheek.

"I can't believe…" he began.

"What?" she asked again.

"That it's so easy for me to trust you." His voice came out gruff-sounding, betraying way more emotion than he liked to let anyone see. He took a curl of her hair from the pillow between them and wrapped it in a ring around his finger.

"And that's strange," she said, "that you feel you can trust me?"

He studied her face in the glow from the lamp. "I'm not real big on trusting people, not right out of the gate like I've been with you." He chucked her under her determined-looking chin. "It's that wide smile, I think. That all-American girl thing you've got going."

She laughed. The sound pleased him. Everything

about her pleased him. "I look trustworthy, is that what you're saying?"

It was more than that, more than he knew how to tell her. So he settled for, "Trustworthy. That must be it."

She reached up and idly combed the hair at his temples with her fingers. Her whiskey-brown eyes were soft with what might have been tenderness. Or maybe understanding.

"You don't reveal a lot," she said. "Tonight, at dinner, I talked about my family and Max. Helen and Mori went on about their children. You were right there in the conversation, interested. And involved. But I noticed you didn't say anything about *your* family."

"You were observing me." He gave her a cool look.

She only grinned. "Yes, I was. I like observing you. I like everything I see."

What did she want to hear from him? "I told you about my mom and dad, remember?"

"Mmm-hmm."

"They died so long ago." He unwound the curl of her hair from his finger. It fell in a soft coil to the pale, perfect skin of her shoulder. "And I've mentioned to Helen—and even to Mori, I think—that they're gone. It didn't seem necessary to tell you what you all already know. I don't have brothers or sisters, so I can't talk about them. And I have no children. So I don't have a whole lot to say when people get going on their families."

"Hmm. Well, yes. That all makes perfect sense...." She was frowning, the smooth skin between her brows crinkling in the cutest way.

He leaned close and kissed her, a quick one, on the end of her nose. "But?"

"I'm greedy, I guess. I want to know everything. All your secrets." She frowned. "Does that sound hopelessly pushy and a little bit scary?"

"Scary, no. Pushy? Oh, yeah."

"Well, okay then. How about this? Anything you want to tell me, I can't wait to hear."

"Shelly…" He kissed her again. This time on the lips. Hard and quick. He couldn't get enough of kissing her. Of touching her. He wanted to tell her… More than he should. About his life, about all the times he'd started over and why. At the same time, he didn't really understand why he even considered revealing all that. Sad stories from the past were better forgotten—or at least, not dredged up while a man was in bed with a desirable woman.

She turned on her side and rose up on an elbow, so she faced him. He knew she longed to prompt him, to beg him to go on. He could see that so clearly in those big brown eyes of hers. But she knew that wouldn't be right.

And in the end, he was absolutely certain she only wanted to know what he was willing to tell her, to share with her.

Now, *that* was strange. He wasn't real big on sharing. He'd learned not to open himself up too much. It only made it hurt more when things went bad, which they always seemed to do in the end. The day always came when he had to move on.

Would it come to that this time? He sure as hell hoped not. He liked Chicago, liked TAKA-Hanson. And he loved his work. The job fascinated him. It was never boring, kept him on his toes.

Plus, now there was Shelly. She was the kind of woman who made a guy want to stick around.

"Hello?" Shelly called softly. "Anybody in there?"

He kissed her smooth forehead. "Sorry. Just thinking— Where was I?"

"Hmm. Let's see. I was being pushy and trying to learn all your secrets. And you started to say something…"

He laughed. "And then I didn't."

"Not yet, anyway."

Really, it *was* better if he didn't get into the past. Instead, he gave her another truth, one that was a whole hell of a lot easier to reveal. "I envied you tonight, all three of you. When Mori and Helen were talking about their family. When you mentioned Max."

She took his hand, turned it over, traced one of the lines at the center of his palm. "Call me Madame Shelly. I see by this line here that you're destined to have many children."

"Oh, yeah?"

"Mmm-hmm. At least a dozen. It says right here."

"I didn't know you read palms."

"I have so many talents. There's no way you'll ever discover them all."

"I plan to work on that. Hard."

"Oh, I'll bet." She said it teasingly—and then her mouth went soft and serious. She laid her palm against his. It felt good there, skin to skin. "You really want kids, huh? I mean, tonight, you felt jealous when everyone was talking about family. And there was last week, too, after Verna's party, when you told me you always wanted kids."

"Yeah?"

"You seem so sure you'll never have them."

"It's not that."

She pressed her lips into his hand. "Then what?" He felt her breath across his palm. She lifted her head, captured his gaze. "What?"

And he realized right then he was going to do it, going to tell her one of the secrets he'd held back a moment before. It was the most painful one, the one that caused him the deepest regret. "I almost had a child once—or at least, I might have had a child. My girl-friend was pregnant. We were having problems. And she…terminated the pregnancy."

"Oh, Tom. Without telling you?"

"She told me after the fact. When it ended between us. By then, it had been a few weeks since she…did it."

She bit her soft lower lip. "How that must have hurt you…"

Again, he considered explaining the bigger picture, telling her about Thatcher, going all the way back to his own disgrace and downfall. But not now. Now, it was way more information than she needed, more than he could bear for her to know. Yeah, something about her made him want to trust her all the way, with every-thing.

Still. No.

He said carefully, "I was…out of work for a while. That caused a lot of tension between us. And then I told her I had to relocate. I had an offer for a good job in New York. We were living in Dallas, which was where we had met. She had her family there. And she loved her own job. And, well, as I said, she and I weren't getting along very well by then. When it ended for good, we had a hell of a fight. She let it out then, that she'd been pregnant. And that she wasn't anymore. She said she just couldn't keep the baby. She couldn't do it alone. And she'd known I was leaving her. So she got rid of it."

"I'm…so sorry, Tom."

He laughed, a dry sound with little humor. "Yeah. Well. Me, too."

"She had no right to do that without consulting you."

He fell back on the pillows and shut his eyes. "But she did. And she was right."

"No…"

"I mean, she had it right that I was leaving. I would have left even if she'd kept the baby. And since she refused to come with me, we never would have been…a family. You know?"

"That's not true. You and your child, you would have been a family."

He thought of her son. "I didn't mean that you and Max weren't—"

"I know you didn't. Life's…strange. Choices get made, and you have to learn to get past them. You have to go on."

"Yeah. Well, and that's what I did. I went on. To New York. And later, to Chicago."

"I can't even begin to tell you how glad I am that you moved to Chicago."

"So am I. Especially tonight, I'm glad. Very, very glad."

She leaned over him, laid her soft fingers against the side of his face.

He grunted. "I need a shave, huh?"

She shook her head and the curving ends of her hair touched his shoulder, soft and light as feathers. Her breasts pressed into his arm, so firm and ripe. He felt himself getting hard again, from the touch of her hair on his skin, from the tempting pressure of those pretty breasts. She said, "I love the feel of you."

He answered roughly, "It's mutual, trust me."

"I like your face all warm and scratchy with your end-of-the-day beard. Lately—the last week or so—I've imagined the two of us, like this. I've fantasized about being able to touch you openly...."

"Incredible." He gave her a slow grin.

"What, that I want touch you?"

"No, that I've been wanting to touch you, too. Touch you everywhere."

"No kidding?" She didn't look especially surprised. In fact, she looked pretty damn confident in her power to drive him crazy with lust. He could hardly blame her, since he'd been making his interest more than clear since that night in front of the Newberry.

"Kiss me," he said. It was a command.

She gave him her mouth. She tasted so good—womanly. Warm. And then, beneath the sheet, her hand found him. She stroked him and he hardened all the more, thickening and growing in her grip. She seemed to like that. From her throat came a low, satisfied sound. Like a purr. Only sexier.

He groaned. "Again?"

So sweetly, she answered, "Well, that would be very nice. But if you're too tired…" While under the sheet, her soft hand was driving him wild.

He made a guttural, animal noise as he strove to remember how to form words. "Never…too tired for you…"

She kissed him again, opening those beautiful lips for him, giving him her tongue as, beneath the covers, she did amazing things with that hand of hers. He went with it, drinking the kiss from her open mouth, moving his body in time to the clever rhythm of her arousing strokes.

The moment came when he had to still her hand— or lose it. He reached down and grabbed her wrist through the sheet, whispered in a voice that could hardly create sound, "Wait. You. I want *you.…* To be inside you."

"Oh, Tom…" She pressed her slim body against him.

"You. Now." He reached for the bed table, fumbling for a condom.

"Please. Let me…" And she helped him, gently pushing his hand out of the way, taking the pouch, getting it open. She peeled the sheet back to reveal him and then she put it on him, rolling it down over the erect length of him, sighing as she did it, making him absolutely certain he was going to explode.

"Now," he muttered. "Shelly. Now…"

And she rose above him, sliding one of those smooth legs across him, giving him a glimpse of sweet pink as she straddled him. He looked up at her and she smiled down at him.

"Now?" she asked, her face flushed with wanting, a knowing smile curving those full lips of hers.

"I know you heard me. You know what I want." He took her by the twin curves of each hip and pulled her down onto him, hard, rising up to meet her, filling her to the limit.

They both groaned then.

And after that, he didn't think. He only felt. Every stroke, every pulse, drowning him, killing him. She was all around him, taking him so deep, all the way to the core of her.

And he was lost. Out of control. Slam-dancing on the outer edge of the universe.

He hit the peak, holding her hips tight as he surged up into her. Behind his eyes, sparks cascaded. She cried out and he felt her body pulsing around him. She was coming, too.

Forever. It went on forever, that climax. Her body contracted around him, demanding all he had to give.

And he gave it. Willingly. As pleasure exploded along every nerve and his body turned itself inside out.

When it was finally over, they drifted, together, falling slowly, weightlessly, back into the world.

He pulled her down, tucked her head against his shoulder, stroked her hair. And then he heard himself whisper, in a tone rough with more emotions than he himself understood, "I trust you, Winston. Who knew, huh?"

"I'm so glad," she whispered back, and lifted her head enough to press her warm lips against his shoulder. "Trust is important."

"Trust is everything. I need to know you'll never betray me."

Her eyes met his directly. Honestly. "Never," she vowed.

He knew she spoke truthfully. "Good." He tipped up her chin and pressed a kiss to her soft lips.

Chapter Seven

Their plane left early, so they had to be up and dressed well before dawn. They climbed out of the big bed at four.

Shelly looked at the tangled sheets and wanted to climb right back in there—and drag Tom in with her. She wanted to wrap herself around him and drift right back into lullaby land.

"Sleep," she teased him groggily. "I didn't get any. Not that I'm complaining—because I'm so not. I mean, other than the fact that I think I might have pulled ten or fifteen muscles in my back, I feel amazing."

"Hurts?" he asked in a tender tone.

"I think I need to have sex more often, give those lazy muscles a regular workout."

"I'll be glad to help you with that. Anytime."

"I knew I'd be able to count on you."

"You can sleep on the plane," he promised her, and he kissed her.

She savored that kiss, as she had every other kiss. As she would each kiss to follow. She hoped there would be many. Thousands. Millions. "Mmm. You are the best kisser. Do that again."

So he did. When he lifted his head that time, he said ruefully, "But we'd better get going…"

She sighed. "Okay, okay. I'm on it. I'll just limp on back to my room and jump in the shower. Ready in twenty minutes."

Helen and Mori were supposed to join them in the company jet, but Helen called Tom while they were in the car on the way to the airport.

"Everything okay?" Shelly asked, when Tom clicked off the BlackBerry.

"It's Kimi."

"Mori's daughter by his first marriage. Right?"

"Right. Something's gone wrong at school again."

"Again?"

"Long story. Kimi's been in a lot of schools."

"But is she okay?"

"Helen says she's fine. Just in another jam. Kimi's continually trying to prove that the system favors the privileged. This time it's an opinion piece she wrote for the college newspaper. The piece suggested that the dean of the business college there is on the take, accepting payment from students and giving out good grades in exchange."

"Yikes."

"Don't worry. It'll work out. Somehow, it always does. But Helen and Mori left for Pennsylvania last night to deal with the problem."

"So…we'll have the jet to ourselves?"

He nodded. "That's right."

Having the jet to themselves…

That could be interesting. Shelly had heard the stories of people who had sex in the air, the so-called Mile-High Club. She'd never thought of herself as someone who might someday be a member.

The idea made her smile.

But then they boarded and there was the pretty flight attendant, who would be right in the cabin with them through the flight. Even if they went into the sleeping alcove and pulled the divider shut, the woman wouldn't have a lot of trouble figuring out what they were doing.

Would that be…tacky? It would certainly be unprofessional. No question about that.

Once they were in the air, Tom took her hand. "Come on." He led her into the sleeping area and pulled the shades down over the windows. She sat on the bed and thought about making love with him, right there, with the attendant on the other side of the thin partition.…

And that got her thinking about the two of them, about how different their relationship had become in the space of one night.

"I've never been the secretary of someone I was sleeping with before," she told him.

He knelt and slipped off her shoes. Then he rose and guided her legs up, onto the bed. "Lie down."

She stretched out on her back and he sat on the edge of the bed, beside her. His eyes had shadows under them. "You look tired."

"I'm fine." He bent close, brushed a kiss against her lips. When he sat up again, he said, "Nothing will change at the office. I promise you. It'll be strictly business there."

She reached for him. He bent closer and she touched him, caressed the side of his face, smooth now from his morning shave. "I think it has to change, at least in some ways."

"And that upsets you?"

"Funny. But it doesn't. Not anymore. You said you trust me…."

"I do."

"I trust you, too. Whatever happens with us, I know you'll treat me fairly. That's the kind of man you are."

He frowned. "What's going to happen? Please. Tell me now."

She chuckled. "Nothing but good things, I'm sure of it."

"That's what I like to hear." He bent close again, kissed her forehead. "Now, get some sleep."

She offered her mouth and he brushed his lips across it. "And here I was picturing myself joining the Mile-High Club."

"Next trip."

"Well, all right."

He rose and stared down at her, his gaze soft and warm. "You can hardly keep your eyes open. Sleep."

"Mmm…" She let her eyelids drift shut. Sleep crept over her. She surrendered to it.

* * *

If they stopped to refuel in San Francisco, Shelly slept right through it. She didn't wake until they'd landed in Chicago and she found Tom leaning close again.

"Wake up, sleepyhead. We're home."

Groggily, she pushed herself up to a sitting position. "Uh…what time…?"

"We gained several hours. It's a little past noon."

"Still Sunday, right?"

"That's right. Hungry?"

"Very."

"Let's eat. I know a great place…."

So they collected their bags and headed for the waiting car. Tom directed the driver to a place he knew in the Loop, not that far from his apartment. Inside the restaurant, it was all Formica and chrome. Retro modern.

The diner offered breakfast all day and the coffee was excellent. Shelly chowed down with enthusiasm.

"Come over to my place," he said when they were done eating, sitting there in the blue vinyl booth savoring a final cup of coffee.

"I'd love to. Truly."

"Am I hearing a 'but' in there somewhere?"

"I need to get home, get groceries, do the laundry…"

"All that can wait."

"No, it really can't. Max is coming home on Tuesday. And the sad truth is, when he's gone I let the fridge go empty a lot of the time. Right now, half a bottle of cranberry juice is keeping lonely company with a bunch of celery and a carrot or two."

"Your refrigerator sounds like mine."

"I need to stock up, get the house in order. Tomorrow's a workday. If I don't do it now, there won't be time. Unless I stay up all night tomorrow night dealing with it."

"All right, all right. I get it. You should go home. How's Max getting here?"

"My mom will drive him up. Another reason I want the place in order. She's staying for the week."

"I get to meet your mother?"

She beamed at him. "I like how you seem so happy about that. I already invited her to the big company picnic on the Fourth." The picnic, which Verna had said was an annual deal, would be held in Grant Park, near the ball fields south of East Balbo Avenue, where they wouldn't be competing with the Taste of Chicago festival happening all week in the northern half of the park.

"Can't wait," he said. "I mean that."

Shelly reached across the table. He met her halfway. They sat there, hands clasped, gazing into each other's eyes as if they were the only two people in the world.

Shelly was barely in the front door when the phone started ringing.

Max. She listened to a detailed report of his activities in the past few days and he told her that he was going to miss his Granny's house, but he was okay with coming home. His friends at KinderKid Daycare would probably be missing him. She told him she loved him and couldn't wait to see him. Her mom came on at the end and asked her how the trip had gone.

"Mom, it was amazing. I didn't get to do much sight-seeing. It was work and more work. But we had the company jet all to ourselves both going and coming. And Tom took me out to dinner with Helen Taka-Hanson and her husband."

"You sound so happy, honey."

"Oh, Mom. I am. I love this job."

"I'm glad," said Norma. "Life is best when you're in love."

"Wait a minute. I said I love my job."

"I'm your mother. I can tell there's something going on."

"Oh, Mom. You're a hopeless romantic."

"I am and proud of it."

Shelly floated through the day on her own special cloud. Doing laundry, dusting the furniture and buying groceries had never been so much fun before. Her mind was filled with Tom and that made even the most mundane chores a joy.

In the morning when Tom arrived at the office, she was at her desk and had been there for an hour, catching up after Thursday and Friday away.

"Shelly," he said with brisk a nod.

"Tom." She gave him her most businesslike smile.

"Fifteen minutes. We'll go over the calendar." He disappeared into his office and she realized she was staring dreamily into space. She shook herself and told her mind to behave.

The display on her phone lit up. It was Tom. She punched his line. "Yes?"

"Shelly, could you come in here, please?" His voice did the naughtiest things to her nerves.

"Sure." She rose and went in.

He stood behind his desk, wearing a dove-gray shirt she particularly admired. Already, he was out of his jacket, in his shirtsleeves. She thought he looked handsomer than ever. If such a thing was possible.

"Close the door, please." His deep voice vibrated with sensual promise.

And though she'd only been his lover since Saturday night, she knew that look in his eyes. It made her stomach all fluttery and her knees go to jelly. With great care, she turned and pushed the door closed. The latch clicked.

He said, "Come here."

She faced him again, but didn't move toward him. Instead she hung back at the door, her hand on the knob behind her. "I don't know. Something tells me what you're planning to do next won't be the least bit professional."

A corner of his mouth quirked up. "You're right. It's not. Come here."

"We agreed to keep things professional here at work."

"You are so right. Come here."

She just couldn't resist him. She let go of the doorknob and raced to him on feet that hardly touched the hardwood floor.

He stepped out from behind the desk and gathered her close. She buried her head in his shoulder. He felt so warm and strong. And he smelled so good.

"You make me crazy, you know that?" His voice vibrated with longing.

She tipped her head back to look at him. "I so relate. I truly do. Because I feel exactly the same about you."

"I want to kiss you."

She reminded herself—again—about the whole sticking-to-business-at-the-office thing. But all she said was, "Oh, yes…" on a heartfelt sigh.

His mouth came down and settled on her in a kiss that swiftly turned blazing hot. He speared his tongue between her eager lips and she wrapped hers around it. Oh, he tasted as good as he felt…

It took just about all of her swiftly fading determination to pull away. "I'm serious." She put a whole lot of effort into trying to sound stern. It was wasted effort. She didn't sound stern in the least. She sounded breathless and hungry for another kiss. "We shouldn't…"

"Yeah," he said gruffly. "We should." He tried to claim her mouth again.

She turned her head so his lips brushed her cheek instead. "Tom. I mean it. Here at the office, we need to stick to business."

"This is business. Serious business."

"This is risky business, that's what this is."

"Look at me."

"Tom…"

"Look at me."

With a sigh of surrender, she turned her face to his.

"Much better." And he kissed her again, a kiss that lasted even longer than the first, long enough to melt her midsection and turn her mind to mush.

When he lifted his head the second time, all she could do was whisper, "Please…"

"My thoughts exactly."

"Oh, Tom…" She stroked his broad shoulders, ran her hands up to clasp him around the neck.

"Do you know how much I've missed you since you left me yesterday morning?"

"I can guess. Since I missed you, too."

His lips were a breath's distance from hers. "You didn't happen to lock the door, did you?"

"Oh, well. I… No. No, I didn't. Because I thought, at the office, we were keeping it strictly—"

"Shh…" His lips met hers for a third time and he waltzed her backward to the door, kissing her passionately the whole way.

When they got there, she heard the lock click behind her as he engaged it. And then he was turning her, guiding her to the caramel-colored sofa along the wall. He edged them in, between the sofa and the coffee table, and then he was guiding her down onto the caramel cushions.

She lay there, pliant, yearning, as he began to undress her.

He had her sleeveless dress unzipped and falling down her arms when he said, "I like this dress. I'll like it off you even better…. Lift up."

With a sigh, she lifted her arms and rose up enough that the dress freed itself of her hips.

And all of a sudden, she was sitting on his office couch in her underwear and her low-heeled pumps. "I don't believe I'm doing this," she whispered, as he smoothly unclasped her bra and took it away, as he dispensed with her half slip and her panties. She hadn't worn pantyhose that day, so she was left sitting there naked, in her shoes.

She said, "You know, you've got a meeting with Helen at ten."

"I know. Shh…"

"But you should—"

"Shh…"

He slid a hand down the back of her calf, causing goose bumps to flare behind her knee and making her exclaim breathlessly, "Oh!" He removed her left shoe and repeated the process with her right.

She looked down at herself. "All of a sudden, I'm totally naked."

"Yeah. You look great this way." He sat back to admire his handiwork. "Maybe we'll start doing the calendar with you naked, put a whole new slant on the workday."

"You are a bad man. A very, very bad man."

He laughed, and took a condom from his pocket. "You have no idea." He set the pouch on the edge of the coffee table. "Since about the third day after you started working for me, while Verna was still here, I've been picturing you on this couch, naked. The fantasy was incredible. The reality? Better." He reached for her.

She put up a hand. "Wait."

He groaned. "I don't know if I can. And don't forget, I've got a meeting at ten."

"My turn." She reached for the knot of his beautiful tie.

"Fine. All right. Do it. Fast."

So she undressed him. She unknotted his tie and slid

it from around his neck, unbuttoned his shirt and took it away to reveal his sculpted chest and that glorious trail of silky hair pointing downward to the tempting bulge at the front of his blue pinstripe slacks. She removed his shoes and his socks.

By the time she got to his Italian leather belt, he forgot all about his promise to wait and reached for her again and started kissing her wildly, so she was forced to get his belt off and his zipper down while he was busy licking his way along her neck and capturing the hard nipple of a breast.

She moaned as he suckled her. His tongue stroked her. She let her head fall back with a hungry cry and tried her best to keep focused on the task at hand. Determined, she eased a hand under the elastic of his boxers and found him.

He was the one who moaned then. She wrapped her fingers around him and stroked him, but his slacks and underwear were in the way. So she urged him to lift up and he did, enough that she could ease his boxers over his lovely, thick arousal, and get everything past his hard hips and halfway down his thighs. He did the rest, shoving them to the floor and kicking them away.

Beyond the locked door, her phone started ringing. He grabbed her closer, until her senses were filled with the feel and the smell and the touch of him....

The phone kept ringing.

She whispered, "I should get that."

"Don't you dare," he growled against her throat. And then he kissed her there, a wet, sucking kiss that sent hot arrows of need shooting through her, a kiss that would leave a love bite, which she would have to be careful to cover with makeup.

She didn't care. Not right then. She didn't care about the phone ringing, or the fact that she was naked in her boss's office, behaving in a manner that could only be called unprofessional. She didn't care about anything at that moment, save the feel of his hands on her, the touch of his lips on her skin, the wet stroke of his tongue wherever he chose to use it.

He caressed her belly and laid her back against the arm of the sofa. And then he kissed her, a hot trail of kisses down the center of her body, all the way to the place she craved him the most. He lifted her right leg and braced it on his broad shoulder and he went on kissing her, wet, thrilling kisses—until she felt herself reaching, climbing toward the peak.

She lost the hot touch of his mouth and she moaned in protest as he rose up above her, one knee in the cushions, the opposite foot braced on the floor. He had the condom, unwrapped, in his hand and he rolled it down over himself. She reached for him, guided him where she yearned for him to be.

After that, she knew nothing but the lift and fall, the rise and retreat, the lovely wet, hot glide of his body within hers. She must have cried out at some point, because he covered her mouth so gently with his hand as he plunged deep within her.

He whispered, "Shhh…Shelly. Oh, yeah, like that…"

He kissed her when he climaxed, using the hot pressure of his mouth on hers to keep himself from crying out. It was a good thing, too, because she was also rising to completion, tightening around him, a hard moan rising from her throat as she hit the crest and slid on over it, into a long, hot shimmer of shuddering fulfillment.

She forgot everything. There was only the pleasure her body was taking from his.

When she came back to herself, he was tracing his tongue around the curve of her ear. He took her earlobe between his teeth and worried it lightly. She moaned softly at the pleasure the teasing kiss gave her.

They lay all tangled together and her head had kind of scrunched down off the couch arm and into the cushions. Not that she cared. She stroked his bare, muscled back and licked a drop of sweat from his cheek.

"I can't believe what we just did," she whispered.

By way of an answer, he made a low, rough, satisfied, extremely masculine sound deep in his throat.

She managed to extricate her left arm from the tangle of body parts so she could look at her watch. "Oh, God. Nine-twenty-two. We need to get to work."

He nuzzled her shoulder, opening his mouth on her skin, teasing her with the wet touch of his tongue. "You taste so good—smell good, too. Better than anyone. They should bottle you. I could pour you all over me."

Beyond the door, her phone started ringing again.

He groaned. "All right, all right. I'm letting you up. Now." He slid one leg to the floor and pushed himself up, one knee still on the cushions.

She gazed up at him, so gloriously naked above her, and she wanted to forget all about that ringing phone, to grab him and pull him back down tight against her and start what they'd just finished all over again.

He said gruffly, "If you look at me like that, we'll never get any work done."

She threw an arm across her eyes. "Get dressed. Do it now."

Tom let her use his private restroom to freshen up. She took extra care to cover the faint mark on her neck.

And fifteen minutes later, she sat, fully dressed, her hair combed and her expression serene, in a chair facing Tom's wide desk. They went over the calendar, moving things around as they needed to in order to get back on track after most of last week away.

He left to meet with Helen at five to ten. He didn't return before lunch. Shelly fielded his calls and got closer to catching up on her own workload.

Finally, after two, he dropped in to pick up messages. She asked him how things had worked out with Kimi.

He chuckled. "Well, they didn't kick her out of the college yet, so that's something." And then he headed for another meeting.

At five, he appeared once more. "Five minutes," he said as he passed her desk. "And then I'll need you in my office."

"Um. Sure."

Without another glance her way, he went in and shut the door behind him.

Shelly smoothed her hair. Well, at least she'd gotten a lot of work done while he was in his meetings. And it *was* the end of the day, after all. They certainly had time for one more amazing encounter on the caramel-colored sofa before heading home. She felt a smile bloom wide across her mouth just at the thought.

But instead of demanding that she lock the door, he glanced up from his computer and asked, "How about dinner?" Before she could answer, he added, "And don't tell me you've got to clean the house. I know that's already handled."

She approached his desk. Slowly. When she got there, she leaned close and said, "Dinner sounds great to me."

They went out for Italian and then they went to his place, which was every bit as sleek and modern as Shelly had imagined it would be. A corner apartment, it had great views of the park. You could even see a sliver of Lake Michigan from the dining area, the water shining in the city lights beyond Lakeshore Drive.

Not that he gave her a lot of time to enjoy the view. Within ten minutes of getting in the door, he had them both naked, stretched out on his king-size platform bed.

The lovemaking they shared was as passionate and fulfilling as the office encounter that morning. Afterward, she lay in his arms and considered the possibility of drifting off to sleep and not waking up till the morning sun came pouring in his floor-to-ceiling windows.

But no. She didn't even have her toothbrush with her. And in the morning, she'd need a change of clothes.

He seemed to sense the direction of her thoughts, because he whispered, "Stay the night…."

She pulled him closer. He laid his head on her breasts and she stroked his thick dark hair. "Can't. I need to get home, for a hundred boring reasons we don't even need to go into."

He lifted up above her so he could gaze down into her eyes. "Tomorrow Max and your mom arrive."

"Mmm-hmm." She reached up to brush the hair at his temples and thought how she would probably never get enough of touching him.

"What time will they get there?"

"Probably late afternoon. For sure, before I get home from the office. My mom will be bustling around putting dinner together. She loves to cook—comfort food, you know? Give her a can of mushroom soup and a pound of frozen broccoli and she'll amaze you with what she can whip up."

"She sounds like a great mom."

"She is. The best."

He ran the back of his finger down the side of her neck, setting off little explosions of pleasure along the surface of her skin. "I can't wait to get to know her and Max. Too bad they're bound to have an adverse effect on my opportunities to get you naked."

She made a low sound of amusement. "Consider it a whole new challenge. You high-powered executive types always love a challenge, right?"

He kissed her chin. "A challenge is good. You naked is better."

In the light from the lamp, the tiny scar over his left eye shone pearly white. She traced it with her finger. "I've been wondering where you got this."

"Swordfight."

She rolled her eyes. "Come on."

"A battle to the death with the evil ruler of an alternate universe?"

She grunted. "If your career in finance ever goes up in smoke, you should consider trying your hand at adventure novels."

"Hmm. A novelist. I like that sound of that...."

She made an effort to look stern, an expression which was seriously hindered by the fact that she was naked and he was cupping her left breast. "Tell," she whispered, touching the small scar once more. "Please."

"You're cute. Even when you're bossy." He fell back to his side of the bed and gazed up at the recessed lights in the high ceiling.

Unwilling to be put off, she nudged him in the side. "Tell."

"Okay, it was like this. I was seven. My mom was out in her garden. She always kept a garden, grew tomatoes and cucumbers, strawberries. String beans. She was big on canning, I remember. And baking. I thought she was the greatest, you know?"

Shelly made a small sound of agreement, pleased to hear the fondness in his voice when he spoke of his mom.

He went on. "Even then, I knew she was older than the other kids' moms. She looked older, kind of tired. Her dark hair was more than half gray. But when she would look at me... Pure love. I think that's everything to a kid. That his mom loves him, that his dad pays attention. And they did. Both of them. They had each other. And me. And that was enough, even though money was always short. Even then, at seven, I remember I wanted to do them proud...."

"And you did," she softly reminded him, laying her hand on his chest.

He put his hand over it, gave a gentle squeeze. "No," he said. "I didn't make them proud. In the end, I didn't make them proud in the least."

Chapter Eight

Something in Tom's voice broke her heart right in two, even though she didn't have a clue what he might mean by what he'd just said.

No. I didn't make them proud.

The words were heavy with pain. And longing. And regret, too.

Regret for what, exactly?

Shelly lifted up on an elbow and gazed down into his eyes. He stared back at her, unblinking. She had no idea what he might be thinking—only that he seemed to be studying her.

"You didn't make them proud? I don't get it. They loved you, you said. And even by the time they died, you had come so far in life. Oh, Tom. I don't understand…."

He glanced to the side then. When he looked back at her, she had the strangest sense that an important moment had just slipped by. He smiled. A hank of her hair had fallen forward.

He caught the curl in his fingers and tugged on it. "Hey. Lighten up."

"But you seemed so…sad, just then."

He guided the strands back over her shoulder. "It's nothing. I exaggerated. They died too soon for me, that's all."

Was it all? She didn't think so. But she remembered her promise of the other night, in the Kyoto hotel room. She wanted to hear any secrets he was ready to share with her. But she wasn't going to push him, as tempting as that might be. In some ways, she felt as if she'd known him forever, as if she'd only been waiting for him to finally show up in her life.

But she couldn't go jumping too far, too fast. They both needed time, together, to *really* learn to know and understand each other.

It seemed to her a great adventure, these first awkward, thrilling steps toward what might someday be love. No, she wasn't like her mother. She didn't jump from attraction to love. But over time, as trust and respect continued to grow between them, well, she would call it love then, and proudly.

And on the subject of trust, what about Uncle Drake? The uncomfortable question popped, uninvited, into her mind.

Now she and Tom were growing closer, now he'd told her he trusted her, why shouldn't she share with him the odd way she'd come to apply for the job as his assistant? Why shouldn't she just go ahead and get it off her chest?

Tom grinned up at her. "What?"

She blinked—and grinned back. "Not a thing."

In the end, what was Drake to her? She'd never set eyes on him in her life except for that one night when he'd popped up out of nowhere and taken her to dinner. He'd said on the phone that he would call and collect some sort of favor. But it had been two weeks since then.

He hadn't called. He might never call.

Right now, there was simply no need to speak of the man. Why take the chance, however small, of ruining everything?

Uh-uh. She would stick with the plan and keep her mouth shut about her uncle until she saw some reason the truth needed to come out.

She kissed Tom's hard, warm shoulder. "So. Back to your mom and her garden and how you got that little scar above your eye…"

His smile made her heart turn over. "After all this buildup, it's pretty anticlimactic."

"Not to me, it won't be."

"Don't be so sure."

"It's about you, isn't it? Nothing about you is anti-climactic."

"Well, it is true. I'm pro climax all the way."

"Okay. Groaning at that one. And not with pleasure."

"Hey. You started it."

"The scar," she insisted. "Your mother. Her garden."

"All right." He sighed. "She was out in the yard, on her knees in the vegetable garden, digging with a red-handled spade and one of those metal clawed hand rakes, to break up the soil. I could see her out there through the sliding-glass door. I had something to show her. I don't know…a picture I'd drawn or homework I'd finished. I slid open the door and called her. She got up and turned to me, smiling, holding the spade. I went running out there to show her what I'd done. Somehow, I tripped on the hand rake. It popped up and bopped me a good one, the claws digging into my forehead, one of them slicing me open right there over my eye. Blood everywhere. I remember I was screaming. I think it scared me more than it hurt. She scooped me up in her arms and took me inside and patched me up, gave me a Tootsie Pop—a grape one. My favorite. For a few days, I had my head wrapped in a white bandage. I considered it to be way cool-looking. All the other kids in the neighborhood were jealous." He shrugged. "And that's it. That's all. The cut over my eye must have been deep enough to leave a scar."

She bent close and kissed it. "It's very…intriguing, a scar on a man."

He grunted. "Not when you get them by tripping on a hand rake."

She kissed him again. "I hate to, but I have to go…."

As usual, he insisted on calling her a cab. She rode home through the nighttime streets, thinking that she'd never been so happy in her life.

In the morning, after they'd finished the calendar, Tom told her he had to fly to San Francisco again the next day.

"Since Max and your mom are coming home today, somehow I'll have to get along this trip without you."

She sent him a look from under her lashes. "Okay, I'm torn. You know I want to go with you...."

He shook his head. "I can manage on my own this time. And you should be here, for your family."

"If you're sure..."

"I'm not. But I can deal. You'll stay here."

"Have I told you lately that you're the best boss I ever had?"

"Keep looking at me like that. I'll be ordering you to lock the door and we'll be giving that couch over there another workout."

"Too bad you've got a meeting in ten minutes."

"Too bad I've got meetings all day."

At noon, Shelly and Lil went to O'Connell's. As it turned out, Shelly didn't have to field as many nosy questions as she'd feared she might, since one of the clerks from HR and another secretary from the finance department spotted them in the pub and joined them. Shelly was grateful for the reprieve from Lil's endless litany of who was doing what with whom, alternating with pointed questions about how things were going with the "hunky CFO."

Shelly got back to work at a little after one and by the time she headed home, she was pretty much caught up after the four days away last week. Tom appeared from one of his meetings just as she was getting ready to leave and gladness speared through her, sharp as a bright ray of light.

"Winston," he said, and indicated that she should follow him.

In his office, with the door shut, they shared a long, delicious kiss. It wasn't nearly enough. But it would have to hold them until his return. She laughed at how much she missed him already. It was only a one-day trip, to check in with Riki again. She would see him Thursday. And Friday would be the big Independence Day picnic.

They rode the elevator down together and parted on the Avenue. She tried not to feel down as he put her in a cab and waved her on her way.

Funny, when you were crazy about a man, it almost hurt to be away from him.

But then she got home and fifty pounds' worth of boy came flying at her, calling, "Mom! I'm home. I know you're so glad!" The house smelled of onion-soup-and-green-bean casserole and her mom came in from the kitchen, wiping her hands on a towel, beaming in welcome.

Yeah, she missed Tom, but it sure was great to have her son across the table from her at dinner, his bent-up glasses taped in three places and his hair sticking straight up from the top of his head as it always did.

And there was more. Her mom had whipped up not one, but two of her famous casseroles.

This was the life, all right.

It took an hour to put Max to bed. He had so much to fill her in on. He'd had to let his pollywog go before it finished its transformation into a frog.

"He still had his tail. But, Mom, he was so close!"

Next year, Max said, he and the friends he'd made in Mount Vernon were going to build a fort down by the creek. They already had a secret club. "With a special handshake and everything. No girls allowed—well, except we're going to have a meeting about Janella Trowley."

"Janella Trowley?"

"She's a girl."

"Hmm. Kind of thought she might be."

"She's six like me. She lives two houses away from Granny and Grandpa and she's not so bad, so we might let her in the club. After the vote, I mean."

"It's good, I think, if you open your club up to everyone."

"Mom. Sheesh. It's not a club if everyone can be in it."

"Well, at least this Janella person. You should let her in."

"We'll see. After the vote. Next time I go to Granny's, we'll vote then. Or maybe the guys'll vote without me. It's okay if they do since I won't be back for a while."

"I like your attitude."

He beamed. "Thanks." And then he frowned. "Just wish my pollywog had changed into a frog faster."

Wednesday was an easy day. Shelly was caught up on her own work and her boss was in California.

Tom called twice under the pretense that he needed her to send him certain files. He could just as easily have sent her a text message or an e-mail. But he called.

Which was more than fine with her. Both times, they talked a little longer than necessary about nothing in particular.

The second time he called, she glanced up in the middle of their conversation to find Lil lurking a few feet away, listening in, wearing a smirk on her full, sexy lips. Shelly sat up straighter in her chair and gave Lil a dead-on look that clearly said the other secretary should mind her own business.

With an elaborate shrug, Lil turned away. And Shelly made a mental note to steer clear of the woman from now on. Yes, Shelly wanted to get along with her coworkers, but Lil Todd was just too nosy for Shelly's peace of mind.

At home that evening, Shelly enjoyed her family and admired Max's new glasses. Her mom had taken him to the optometrist, where they'd been waiting to be fitted.

Later, Tom called. Shelly took the phone into her room and they talked for an hour. He told her he and Helen were still seriously concerned about Riki's performance, but willing to stick with the designer for the next few weeks, as previously agreed—and yes, in the meantime, they'd continue the hunt for a possible replacement, just in case.

Thursday afternoon at one, Tom called Shelly on her cell. He'd just touched down at O'Hare. "Winston."

"Yeah?"

"You're the best assistant I ever had."

"Why, thank you, Tom."

"I want you to know how much I appreciate you."

Shelly sat at her desk with a spreadsheet open on the

monitor in front of her. She cradled the phone against her cheek and tried to look professional, though she had no doubt the fool's grin on her face and her dreamy eyes would have been a dead giveaway if anyone was watching.

"I do know you appreciate me. Thank you."

He said, "I think you should take the afternoon off." Did that mean she wouldn't see him till the picnic tomorrow? Her spirits drooped. Then he added, "You should meet me at my place. One hour."

"But—"

"Winston."

"Yes?"

"Never argue with the boss." He hung up.

She set down her phone and stared blankly at her computer monitor. *His place. One hour.*

She was there five minutes early. The friendly doorman must have been warned to expect her. He gestured toward the elevators and called her "Ms. Winston."

At Tom's door, she raised her hand to knock—and the door opened. A strong hand shot out and grabbed her wrist. She laughed as she was pulled into warm, hard arms.

Vaguely, she heard the door swing shut behind her. And then he was kissing her. Madly. Deeply. An endless, tender, passionate kiss.

When they came up for air, he said, "I thought you'd never damn well get here. What is it about you, Winston? Tell me. What?"

But then he didn't let her answer. He only kissed her again and waltzed her into his bedroom and took off all her clothes and his, too.

Later, they lay together in the afternoon light. He told her all about his trip. Then they made love again. And again.

Reluctantly, at five, he sent her home to her mom and her son, promising he'd be at her place the next day to pick her and her family up and take them to the company picnic. Shelly rode home in a warm haze of mingled fulfillment and anticipation.

The next morning, the doorbell rang at eleven-fifteen. Shelly went to answer. Just the sight of the handsome man on her doorstep made her heart skip a beat.

"Good morning." He carried a big bouquet of brightly colored gerbera daisies. "A street vendor was selling them. I made the driver go back so I could get you some...."

She grinned like a long-gone fool and gathered the flowers into her arms. "They're beautiful. Thanks."

"You should put them in water."

"I will. Come in." She stepped back.

Max was lurking behind her in her small entryway. He had his arms folded across his thin chest and a very serious expression on his face. "Hello," he said solemnly.

Tom glanced at Shelly. She gave him a nod. He stepped forward until he loomed over her child. "I'm Tom."

Max gave the man before him a slow, cautious once-over. "Are you my mom's boss?"

"Yes, I am."

"Oh." With great dignity, Max extended his hand. Tom took it. They shook.

When Tom let go, Max said, "I just got back from Mount Vernon. That's where my Granny lives."

Tom nodded. "Your mom told me you'd been gone."

Max tipped his head to the side. "But I bet she didn't tell you *everything*."

Tom took a minute to think about that. "You're right. I'm sure she didn't."

"*I'll* tell you all about it."

"All right. Tell me. I can't wait to hear it all."

Max smiled then—a broad, open smile. "Good." And he started chattering. "Well, first Mom drove me down there. It's a long drive. We get to stop and have hamburgers on the way. I like ketchup on mine. And I like a chocolate milkshake, too. And French fires. But Mom always says I can't have both so I have to choose. I had the French fries that time, on the drive down to Granny's. And milk to drink…"

Shelly clutched her bright flowers. Her chest felt tight. Max's cautious expression had vanished. Now his eyes shone and the tension had left his small body.

Just like that, it had happened. Her son had made his choice and decided to accept Tom into his world.

Uncertainty gnawed at her. It was one thing for her to take a chance on a man, but another altogether to find that her son already trusted him. If things didn't work out between them…

No, she ordered herself silently. *Don't go there. Not now.* It was a sunny summer day, the Fourth of July. A time for fireworks and fun.

Shelly put her second thoughts away.

Max was still talking as Tom listened, rapt. "And then we—"

"Whoa." Laughing, Shelly put up a hand.

Max stuck out his little chin. "But, Mom, Tom wants to know about my trip to Granny's."

"And you'll get to tell him." She sent Tom a you-asked-for-it grin. "But right now, let me introduce him to Granny and then we can be on our way."

Max reached for Tom's hand. "Come on, Tom. Granny's in the kitchen, I think…."

They got to Grant Park at a little after noon.

TAKA-Hanson had taken up a large, grassy area under the shade of some gorgeous old oaks. The picnic tables were covered in red, white and blue cloths, complete with centerpieces decked with American flags and red top hats.

The limo let them off, and Max stared with stars in his eyes. "Wow. This is gonna be some party, huh?"

And it was

There was softball. Tom played first base for the hospitality division team. Shelly, Norma and Max cheered him on. Shelly met Helen's stepsons and their wives and babies.

HR had even hired a band. As the night came on, Shelly and Tom danced together on a wide wooden dance floor that had been set up under the stars.

Later, there were fireworks over Lake Michigan. Tom, Shelly, Norma and Max spread a blanket on the grass and watched the show. Max fell asleep halfway through, his face so angelic and peaceful in the light of exploding bottle rockets and fountains of cascading multicolored fire.

When they got home, Shelly's mom carried Max in

to bed and Tom and Shelly lingered on the front step, sharing kisses as, high in the sky over Chicagoland, more fireworks exploded.

"I promised Max I'd take him to a movie tomorrow," Tom teased before he left. "I said I had to check with you first, though."

A movie? Her son and Tom were already making plans for things they'd do together? Her doubts of earlier that day resurfaced.

A nagging voice in the back of her mind chided that they were moving too fast, that she should tell Tom they needed to slow down....

But when she answered, all she said was, "Hmm. I suppose a movie is fine with me."

"Max said, if I asked you nicely, you might even come with us."

"You know, I just might." Again, she spoke lightly, denying her doubts.

"He also asked for my phone number."

"Don't give it to him," she warned. "He'll be calling you constantly."

"I'll set parameters."

"Oh. Right. Parameters. Of course."

"That is, if it's all right with his mom."

"It's okay with me. Just don't say I didn't warn you."

Tom kissed her again. "I'll check the movie listings in the morning, and give you a call. Invite your mom, too, will you?"

"I will." She stood on the porch and waved as he drove away, her happiness bright as a firework fountain exploding over Lake Michigan in the Fourth of July night.

Yes, alone in her bed that night she worried—a little. That so much was at stake. Not only her heart—and her job. But now her son's heart, as well. If things went bad with Tom...

But then, in the darkness, she smiled. Really, why *not* look on the bright side? Why *not* expect the best?

The next day all four of them went to a feature-length cartoon about a family of dancing hedgehogs. Tom gave Max his cell number and they all went out for burgers after the show.

Sunday, Norma watched Max so that Shelly and Tom could have the afternoon together. By then Shelly's doubts were fading. Really, her life was just about perfect. It didn't get any better than this.

Or maybe it did.

Maybe she and Tom were headed for a future together. It could happen. As each day passed she only became more certain that it *would* happen. She was falling in love with her boss. And she had a very strong feeling he was falling for her, too.

Monday morning, Shelly's mom headed for home. Shelly hugged her goodbye and told her to drive carefully, then took Max to daycare.

She got to TAKA-Hanson at a little before eight. When Tom came in, they went over his calendar. He had some calls to make. And then, about ten-thirty, he hurried off for an emergency meeting with Helen and some of the finance managers.

He didn't return until around two in the afternoon. As he entered his office, he gave her a nod. "Shelly. Do you have a moment?"

"Of course." She got up and followed him in, warmth sifting through her at the naughty idea that perhaps they'd be sharing a tender interlude on the caramel-colored couch.

But then he went and sat at his desk and gestured for her to take a chair.

Aware of a sudden vague sensation of alarm, she took the one she always used when they did the calendar. "Is everything…okay?"

"No. It's not. We have a problem. A serious one. You know Lillian Todd, right?"

"Sure." She kept her personal opinion of Lil to herself. It seemed the most professional approach. "We…chat now and then. Around the water cooler, that kind of thing. We had lunch together at O'Connell's last week, along with a couple of the girls from the office." Shelly frowned. "You know, I haven't seen her today. Is she all right?"

"What I'm going to say is strictly confidential."

Alarm ratcheted higher. "Of course."

"Helen's impressed with you."

Where was this going? "Well. I'm…pleased. I really like her, too."

"She suggested I get your take on this. I agreed that sounded like a good idea."

"Certainly. Whatever I can do." Whatever *this* was…

"I just need it to be crystal clear. Nothing that gets said here can leave this room."

"Absolutely. Strictly confidential. I understand…"

"Lillian Todd didn't come in to work today. We've had a long talk with Louie D'Amitri, the manager she was working for, and we have reason to believe she's been accessing financial files and correspondence that have nothing to do with her job at TAKA-Hanson."

Shelly could hardly believe her ears. "You mean… you think Lil Todd is some kind of spy?"

Tom nodded. "She evidently became intimate with Louie and convinced him to give her his password, which allowed her to access areas of our systems that she never should have been able get near."

Lil? Sexy, man-crazy, gossip-hungry Lil—a *spy?* "It's so hard to believe…."

"Yeah, well. We do believe it. We believe that Lillian Todd has been copying crucial confidential information off our system and passing it to the competition."

"But…how?"

Tom said, "The system keeps track of who uses it, and when. Louie, the poor sucker, is an honest guy at heart. He came to us today, confessed that she'd gotten him to give her his password. Luckily, we've been able to pinpoint what, exactly, she's stolen. Unfortunately she must have figured out she was about to get caught. She's vanished. We've called a detective service we keep on call. They sent a man to her place. It was empty. The manager said she'd moved out over the weekend."

Shelly knew enough about big business to understand that, though a crime had been committed, the police would not be informed. Filing a complaint would mean admitting that TAKA-Hanson had been careless enough to allow its most carefully guarded information to be stolen. No self-respecting corporation wanted that kind of egg on its face.

No. This "problem" would remain in-house. Louie D'Amitri wouldn't even be fired for giving access to the spy. He'd be offered reassignment, for the same money, out of corporate headquarters, where he'd no longer be in the TAKA-Hanson financial inner circle and where he'd have no access to top-secret information.

In other words, the corporate boneyard. No doubt Louie would decline the offer, take a fat severance package and try his luck elsewhere.

Tom said, "And what I called *you* in for…"

"Whatever I can do. Just say the word." She still couldn't believe it. Lillian, a corporate spy? It didn't seem real. Lil, with her sly looks and swaying walk, had been working undercover for some other hotel chain, stealing TAKA-Hanson secrets?

"Since you're clerical," Tom said, "and since I trust you absolutely…"

"Thank you," she told him softly.

His smile was bleak. "We thought you might have heard something—from Lillian herself, or from one of the other secretaries—that management wouldn't necessarily be aware of, something that would help us figure out who she was working for and how to catch up with her."

Shelly carefully considered before she answered. "I just… I didn't know that much about her. I never had her phone number, even. She never mentioned her family, now that I think about it. Mostly, she just gossiped about everyone else in the office."

"A good way to keep anyone from getting too close," Tom remarked.

"Yeah. You're right. And to get information, I suppose. Verna said she was really smart, that she had to be, given that she spent most of her time making the rounds of the office, gossiping, and very little time at her own desk. I mostly felt…cautious around her. I never wanted to tell her anything that she might tell everyone else."

"Smart," he said.

"Simple self-preservation. Oh, and I did hear the rumor that she was sleeping with her boss." Shelly gulped. After all, Lil wasn't the only one who'd been in bed with the boss.

"Who told you she had a thing with Louie?"

Shelly told him the name of the other secretary. "I got the sense it was general knowledge, Lil and Louie. And, well…"

"Tell me. Anything. It just might help."

She warned, "This is totally my take and nothing more."

"Duly noted."

"I… Well, I thought more than once that Lil was interested in you. But why wouldn't she be?" When he arched a brow, she elaborated, "I mean, you're single and handsome and the head of finance. Lil was always so…flirtatious with all the guys. I could see her considering you a big step up from a middle-aged, middle-management married guy—and hey, as a spy, she'd want to get as far up the corporate food chain here as possible, right?" Shelly glanced away. "Gee. Did that sound totally tacky or what?"

"What gave you the idea she was 'interested' in me?"

"Nothing concrete, I promise you."

"Tell me anyway."

"It was only…the way she would look at you—that sexy smile she gave you at the bar during Verna's party. And then, later during the party, after you and I danced, I ran into her in the ladies' room. She got all sly with me, asked me if I was having a 'good time' in this really snarky tone of voice. Then the Wednesday before we flew to Japan, she came by my desk to try and get me to go to lunch with her.

"I was focused on getting caught up before the trip and said I couldn't—oh, and that's another thing. She knew about both trips last week. I hadn't told her about them. Though that's not that big a deal, right? I guess she could have heard about the trips any number of ways, but still… She asked me how I liked working for you. She called you the 'hunky CFO' and, I don't know, she just seemed jealous or something." Shelly blew out a breath. "This is silly. I'm not giving you anything useful. I'm sorry."

He was watching her intently, taking it all in. "Don't apologize. What else?"

"It's nothing."

"Tell me."

"I told her I couldn't go to lunch that day, and suggested we try the next week. She said something like how anything could happen between then and next week. That struck me as odd. Then she shrugged and said 'Why not?' when I said 'How about Tuesday?'"

"Anything else? Whatever you remember."

Shelly shook her head. "I'm sorry. That's pretty

much it. I wish I could be more help, but I had no idea she was up to anything—beyond being a man-crazy gossip. You might try getting hold of Verna and asking her for her take on Lil. Verna dealt with her for a lot longer than I did."

"That's a thought. We want to keep this under wraps as much as possible, though."

"I understand. And I just… It's so strange. I was wary of Lil—suspicious, you know? But never in a million years would I have pegged her for a spy. I guess she totally had me fooled."

"You're not alone. She had everyone fooled."

Chapter Nine

Tom went back into a closed-door session with Helen and his department managers at three. At five, he was still in the meeting. Shelly left the office without seeing him again that day.

Tom called the house around seven, just to check in and to apologize for being preoccupied.

"I get it," she replied. "There is nothing you have to apologize for. This is serious and you've got to deal with it. I only wish I could help."

"You do help," he told her. "Just by...being you."

They talked for a few more minutes and then he said goodbye. She finished cleaning up the kitchen, got Max into his bath, watched the news, put Max to bed. The whole time she was aware of a certain…tension with herself. A sort of irritation, rubbing just beneath the skin.

"I think I'd better call Tom," Max said when she tucked him in for the night.

"Not tonight, big guy. Tom's kind of busy."

"Aw, Mom. Tomorrow?"

"Probably. But check with me for the right time."

Max untangled his arms from beneath the sheet and folded then across his chest. Just to make sure she got the message that he was not pleased, he stuck out his lower lip. "Tom said I could call him."

"And you will—but not if you keep sticking out your lip like that."

"I'm not."

"You are."

"Not."

"Are." Shelly knew how to win the argument. She tickled him.

Max squirmed and laughed and shouted, "Stop, don't. Ouch!"

"Say you'll stop pouting…"

"Awright, okay. I'll stop, I'll stop!"

She quit tickling and looked at him levelly. "And what are the rules about calling people?"

"I have to ask first and not be a pest."

"That's right. So follow the rules. Got it?"

"Yeah."

She kissed him and left, turning out the light, pulling the door silently shut. And then she went around the house locking up, wishing she didn't feel so edgy, wondering how Tom was doing, hoping he'd had a decent dinner and would get a good night's sleep.

A bath sounded like just the thing—a long, lazy soak. She would let the tension of the day seep away into the warm, soothing water.

She put in some bath salts, undressed and sank into the tub with a grateful sigh. Leaning back, she closed her eyes.

And then, a moment later, the nagging feeling that something wasn't right found its focus. She popped up straight. Water and bubbles surged over the tub rim.

"Oh. My. God," she said aloud to the tiled walls that surrounded her. "Uncle Drake..."

Uncle Drake, with his inside information about TAKA-Hanson. Uncle Drake, who'd known that Verna was leaving before anyone else did. How could he have known that?

Through Lil. Oh, God. Through Lil. It made perfect sense.

Lil was working for Drake.

Was that possible?

Shelly knew the answer to that one. In the world of corporate one-upmanship, just about any dirty trick was possible.

It all came so painfully clear. Lil had wanted Shelly's job. Yes. Of course. But Verna hadn't thought much of Lil and had let Lil know—probably with great tact and serious diplomacy—that she wasn't going to get it.

Lil had told Drake. And Drake had passed the tip on to Shelly, figuring that it was better than nothing, to have a niece who owed him a favor in the job, if his spy wasn't going to get it.

But why?

Why would Drake want spies at TAKA-Hanson?

Shelly jumped from the bath, splashing water everywhere. Still soaking wet, with bubbles dripping down her legs, she grabbed her robe and yanked the tie tight around her and hustled into the bedroom where she grabbed her cell. She auto-dialed Tom.

And then she snapped the phone shut before the connection was made.

She pressed the phone to her forehead. "Coward," she whispered. "I am such a coward...."

At last, she had everything. A great job. An amazing man who liked her son. A possible future with the requisite rosy glow all around it.

She was going to lose it all.

She should have told Tom about Drake. She should have told him right at the first.

And lost the job without ever getting it.

Yeah. That's what would have happened. She knew it. She'd known it all along. Men like Drake didn't warn you not to mention their names unless they knew for a fact that it wouldn't go over well.

But she'd lied to herself about what she knew. She'd kept a dangerous secret to protect herself from losing it all. She'd tried to tell herself that everything would be okay, that all she had to do was keep quiet and work hard. All she had to do was bury her nose in the sand and the problem would go away on its own.

Within days of landing the job at TAKA-Hanson, she

had her long-lost uncle pushed, like the darkest of night-mares, into the farthest corner of her mind. Like most nightmares, he would pop up occasionally.

And she would shove him right back down.

Shelly rushed on bare, wet feet into the kitchen where she'd left her laptop when she got home from work. She booted it up. And then she did the thing she should have done weeks ago, the thing she had been avoiding since the night her uncle first appeared in her life.

She surfed the Web for anything she could find about Drake Thatcher.

For half an hour, she waded through endless references to her mother's half brother, most of them to do with his various businesses, more than one implying that he wasn't the most straight-ahead entrepreneur to get a nod in *Business Weekly*.

And then, there it was, a few lines in the "New Projects" section of *Hotelier Monthly Online:*

6/25. Drake Thatcher in the hotel business? So our sources tell us. The wealthy tycoon's newly formed Thatcher Group will be developing top-end luxury hotels. Prospective grand opening of the group's flagship site slated for thirty-six months out in San Francisco. More as the project develops.

Shelley read those lines over twice. And then a third time.

Drake Thatcher in the hotel business.

She'd feared the worst and she'd gotten it. Again, she

grabbed the phone. She dialed the number Drake had given her. Like last time, she got his voice mail. When the line beeped, she babbled out a frantic message.

"Uncle Drake, it's Shelly. I really need to speak with you as soon as possible." She rattled off her numbers—both home and cell. "Please. Call me back as soon as you get this." She hung up and set the phone on the desk next to her computer, half expecting it to ring any second.

It didn't ring. Drake didn't call back. Not that night, or the next morning. Shelly went to work with a hot band of dread squeezing her chest.

Tom came in at the usual time, looking distracted. All night, she'd been telling herself that she'd get honest with him the minute she saw him.

She did no such thing. She greeted him with a casual, "Morning." He responded with a quick, warm smile and went into his office. He left for meetings as soon as they finished the calendar.

Shelly watched him go and despised herself for being a total coward, at the same time as she desperately reminded herself that she'd done nothing wrong, done nothing to compromise Tom or TAKA-Hanson. Nothing except get a mysterious job tip from an uncle she hardly knew. Nothing except keep her mouth shut when Drake called her and said outright that in the future, he would expect her to spy for him.

It was, after all, entirely possible that Lil wasn't working for Drake, that some other company in competition with the Taka hotels had put Lil in place in the finance department.

It *was* possible that Lil had stolen TAKA-Hanson files for someone else altogether. Shelly clung to that, to the faint and fading hope that Lillian Todd and her uncle were in no way connected.

Tom returned at a quarter to five. He called her into his office. "I was kind of hoping we might get together tonight," he said. "Pick up a pizza, go to your place. But it turns out I've got meetings, damn it. This thing with Lil Todd has put us behind. And then there are the endless issues with San Francisco and Kyoto. We need to go over some numbers."

She smiled. "Just please try and get some rest when you get home." Amazing. How sweet and calm she sounded, how little like the two-faced liar she knew herself to be.

"Rest," he said. "I hope. How's Max?"

"Fine. Getting back into his daycare and his buddies here in town."

Tom rose from his desk and came around to her. She stood to meet him. "He wants to call me, right?"

"Does a sea lion poop in the bay?"

He chuckled and put his big hands on her shoulders. She melted inside—hating herself. Wanting him so. He tipped her chin up with a finger and they shared a sweet, soft kiss.

Then he asked, "What time does he go to bed?"

"Around eight-thirty, but you don't have to—"

"Eight-thirty's good. Tell him to call me then...."

"All right. Yes. I will."

He brushed the backs of his fingers along the side of her neck and she wished he would always touch her like that—with such tenderness, such loving care. She wished she might never lose him. That they might always share this closeness.

Maybe they would. He was such a good man. If she told him the truth, chances were he would understand. She should tell him now. Just get the damn words out.

He was frowning. "Winston. You okay?"

And she told yet another lie. "Fine. Truly."

"Good." He kissed her again, a deeper, even sweeter kiss. When he lifted his head, he said, "This weekend, I promise. We'll spend time with Max. And maybe Saturday night, if you could get a sitter…" He let the suggestion finish itself.

"I'll see what I can do."

"It's a deal." And then he let her go.

That night, as she tucked Max in, she handed him her cell.

He reached for his glasses on the nightstand, sat up and pushed the covers back. "Tom?"

She nodded, her throat clutching at the excitement in his voice.

He flipped open the phone and punched out the numbers, fast, from memory. Then he put the phone to his ear and waited, his expression oh-so-serious. She knew when Tom answered because her little boy beamed.

"Hello, Tom. This is Max."

The tight band that seemed to have wrapped itself around her chest lately grew tighter still as she listened to her son tell Tom all about his friends in daycare, about the model of a frontier fort he was making with Popsicle sticks, about the butterfly cocoons incubating in a terrarium in a corner of the daycare classroom.

On top of the tightness in her chest, her throat clutched harder and her eyes burned with unshed tears. So that Max wouldn't see her distress, she rose and went to the window, where she stared blindly out at the twilight and the gray clapboard wall of the house next door. Behind her, Max continued to chatter away.

"Yeah. I can't wait for the butterflies to come out of their cocoons. A cocoon is also called a chrysalis—did you know that, Tom? Or a pupa. Pupa." Max laughed. "That's a funny word, huh? I like the pupas almost as much as I like watching chicken eggs hatch. We did that before I went on my trip to Granny's. I like chicks, little fuzzy yellow balls. My granny has chickens in back of her house. And a big, mean rooster who will peck you if you get too close. … Mmm-hmm. I can. Yeah…"

Lord. They *liked* each other so much, Max and Tom. Right from the first, when Max offered his hand to Tom last Thursday before the picnic, they'd seemed to have a connection. Was that connection in jeopardy now?

"Mom."

She whirled from the window, pasting on a bright smile.

The small hand held out the phone. "Tom wants to talk to you now."

Shelly took the phone. She made all the right noises. She told him she'd see him tomorrow. And then she said goodbye. She kissed her son good-night, shut the curtains, turned out the light and left him, pulling the door closed behind her.

Now what?

Her problem remained the same as it had been from the first. The truth counted, but how much? How much did this particular truth matter, when measured against the terrible damage her revealing it might do—when really, she *was* innocent of wrongdoing. Her uncle had asked her to do nothing unacceptable.

Not yet, anyway.

Maybe he would never ask her—okay, she didn't believe that. But it *was* possible.

She thought of getting ready for bed, of slipping between the cool sheets…

For what? So she could spend the night staring into the darkness, her stomach in knots?

She wandered out to the front porch and sat on the step and watched the twilight fade to true night. Seeking a peace that didn't come, she tried to clear her mind of the truth that dogged her, to simply sit. To simply *be*. Leaning back on her hands, she stared up at the dark sky.

The city lights obscured the stars and planets spinning so far above her head—all but the brightest of them, anyway: the North Star. Mars, maybe. She wished that by staring up at those bright points of light she might find her answer, know what she had to do.

Keep silent and wait? Tell all now and accept the consequences?

No answer came to her.

But then she lowered her gaze and stared out past her

front walk at the street, where a long, black limousine was just then sailing to a stop at the curb. The door opened. Her uncle, in a designer suit of gray silk, leaned out.

"Shelly. Just the woman I wanted to see."

Chapter Ten

Her chest so constricted, it hurt to breathe, Shelly rose from the step and went down the walk to the shining black car.

Drake gave her a nod. "I did get your message. And as it happens, I need to have a little talk with you, anyway."

She glanced over her shoulder at the lights of the house. She couldn't drive off with him and leave Max alone. And she didn't want to ask him in, didn't want to chance her son waking and coming out to see who was visiting his mom.

"My son's in bed. I can't go anywhere."

"No problem. We can talk right here in the car." He slid back along the seat, clearing a space for her.

No. She was not getting into that big car with him and his driver and the too-heavy scent of his expensive cologne.

"Sorry," she said, "but I should stay close to the house. In case my son needs me...."

Drake scowled, but he did emerge from the car. It was then that she noticed he held a large manila envelope in his perfectly manicured hand.

"Let's, um, sit on the porch." She signaled the way up the walk.

He went ahead of her. At her front step, he turned and graced her with an insincere smile.

"Well, I believe congratulations are in order. You have more than exceeded my expectations."

"What expectations? I don't understand."

"Come on, Shelly. You're not stupid. I mean with Tom Holloway. He's hardly a trusting type. But he trusts *you*, doesn't he? Not even a month since you became his assistant and you're spending your nights in his bed, leading the guy around by the nose." She opened her mouth to protest, but Drake only laughed and waved a hand. "Spare me the outrage. I've had you followed. I know everything. I've even got pictures of you going in and out of his apartment building—once at night. And that time during the day last week when you dropped in for a few hours of good, sweaty fun."

Shelly told herself she would not let this man get to her. So what if he knew about her and Tom? She didn't care if he knew. She didn't care if the whole world knew. She was *proud* of her relationship with Tom.

She said coolly, "You talk as if you know Tom personally."

"Maybe that's because I do."

"Excuse me?"

"What? He hasn't mentioned me? I'm crushed. As a matter of fact, Tom and I go way back. He worked for me once. Sadly, that didn't turn out well for him. Small world, no?"

Shelly held herself very still. She had the sense that, if she moved too quickly, she would shatter, just break into a thousand pieces and go flying off in all directions.

Tom had worked for Drake. And something had happened back then, something that had turned out bad for Tom. Oh, God. This was worse. Worse than she'd ever imagined.

She strove to think clearly, to get past her shock and learn whatever she could while she had the chance. Somehow, she forced a tight smile. "Small world. True. And too bad about Lil Todd, huh? I'm guessing she was getting good information for you—until she almost got caught. She's lucky she got away in time."

He shrugged. Elegantly. "Lil Todd? Hmm. I don't believe I know a Lil Todd." The gleam in his eyes told her otherwise.

"I think you're lying, Uncle Drake."

With his free hand, he brushed a nonexistent bit of lint off his beautifully cut sleeve. "Never call me a liar, Shelly. You don't want to get on my bad side, believe me."

What she wanted was to scream at him, to call him names a lot worse than *liar.* But somehow, she held it together. She remained calm. At least on the outside.

Quietly, she asked, "Why are you here?"

"You called me."

"There's more, though. Isn't there?"

"As it happens, there is. I told you I'd be in touch, that eventually I'd need a favor. That time has come." He held up the manila envelope. "As I said, you've done well. Now you're so perfectly in place, I wish we could make better use of you there. But decisions have been made to move ahead and get rid of Tom. So we're running out of time. Your boss's messy past is about to catch up with him. It's all going to come out in the press. The whole sad story. His arrest, his conviction. The unfortunate period in prison. He'll be asked to leave TAKA-Hanson within the week, just watch. And that means you'll be out of a job."

Tom had been in prison? "But…how? Why?"

"It's all in here." He tapped the envelope with a finger. "A little recap, just for you, so you'll understand completely what's really going on here. Inside, you'll find copies of clippings from the *New York Times* and the *Wall Street Journal* detailing the whole ugly mess." He turned the envelope over to reveal a check paper-clipped to the back. Helpfully, he slid the check free of the clip and held it up so she could get a look at all the zeros scrawled across the front. "As you see, it's made out to you. It should hold you over quite nicely until I find you something new."

Information, she reminded herself. *Information is power.* Maybe all was lost between her and Tom. The awful, sinking feeling in her belly told her that when she gave him that folder—which she knew she had to do— he would never trust her again.

Oh, she should have told him about her uncle. She should have told him at the beginning, no matter the cost....

Not the point right now, she reminded herself. *What will happen when I tell him is not the point. The point is to get that envelope before Drake gets back in that car.*

That way, at least, when she told Tom the truth and destroyed all she and Tom had together, she could, just possibly, give him something to go on, something to help him save himself at TAKA-Hanson. She didn't want him ending up like poor Louie, either on the street or farmed out to some job that went nowhere.

She played it for sulky self-interest and muttered, "If I'm going to be out of a job again, I do need that money."

"And it's yours. Of course, I'll expect some immediate return."

She was silent for a count of ten, as if wrestling with her conscience. At last, she said, "Fine. Tell me what I have to do."

He waved the envelope again. "In here, besides the clippings, you'll also find a password my people have managed to acquire. Up to this point, it hasn't been used to raid the TAKA-Hanson system, so it should still be good. I'll need the current files on your division's second phase. Till now, we've been unable to acquire that information. I want to know where they're expanding next, beyond the flagships, and how far along they are. I need to know what builders they've lined up, the suppliers they'll be using, whatever they have going forward, so I can begin to put my people in place where they'll do the most good."

What questions would she ask if she intended to do what he wanted? "You're sure—about the password? If they find out what I'm up to—"

"The password is good. Someone dependable acquired it—just before she was no longer able to gain access to the system." Someone like Lil Todd? Shelly didn't ask. She knew he wouldn't tell her. He said, "You have to move fast. I can't stress that enough."

She swallowed a bleak laugh. She would be getting on it fast, all right. Faster than he knew.

He continued, "Tomorrow, if at all possible, get into the system and get what you can. As soon as Holloway's out of there, you will be, too, and the opportunity will be missed. The system has an excellent firewall and won't allow access by nonrecognized computers. It also won't let you send the information on electronically. So transfer the data to a jump drive or CD. When you've gotten what you can, call the number you have for me and leave a message. I'll be in touch as to what you need to do next."

She nodded. "All right." Was she being too cool for a first-time corporate spy? God. "Um. I...should go." She glanced toward her front door, nervously. "Anything else?"

Drake smiled. She hated his smile almost as much as she hated his damn aftershave. "That's it. Very simple."

Her hands itched to snatch the envelope from him. But somehow, she made herself wait until he handed it over, which he did. At last. She took it with a nod and turned to go up the steps.

He stopped her by grabbing her arm. "You do realize the position you're in, Shelly?"

It wasn't hard in the least to pretend to be terrified. She jerked her arm from his grasp and stammered weakly, "I, um, I..."

"Tom Holloway hates me. I am...the past he never shakes. Your merely being my niece is enough to make you his enemy. If he learned that I was the one who told you to apply for a job as his assistant...he would not be understanding. If he found out that I told you three weeks ago I would expect you to copy company files for me—and you kept silent—he would never forgive you. Am I making myself clear?"

Her throat had locked up. She had to cough to loosen it. "Yes," she croaked. "Perfectly."

"Your best bet here—your *only* bet—is to do what I've told you to do. Cash that check, put food on the table for you and your child. And get me the information I've told you to get."

"I... Yes. I will," she baldly lied. "I'll do what you want."

He was smiling again. "Excellent. Your golden-boy boss isn't who you think he is. Read. Learn. Get back to me as soon as you have my information for me. And have a nice night."

That time when she turned for her door, he didn't stop her. Seconds later, she stood in her front hall, the door firmly shut behind her, clutching the envelope to her chest, waiting for her knees to stop shaking.

As soon as she felt she could walk without her legs giving way, she went to the spare room and shut the door. She sat at the small desk she had in there, laid the envelope on the desktop, facedown, and stared at the check Drake had given her.

Fifty thousand dollars. Evidently, he considered that the price for her betrayal of Tom and TAKA-Hanson, a fair rate of exchange for her integrity and self-respect.

Shelly shook her head. It wasn't enough. No amount would be enough. Some things she would never sell, though she did see now—all of her earlier denials to the contrary—that she *had* done wrong.

She'd let her uncle believe she *might* sell those things and she had lied by omission to Tom. Now it fell to her to do what she could to repair the damage she'd helped to cause. It fell to her to reclaim her own tattered honor.

The cost, she knew, would be great. She would have to give back all she had gained by her own dishonesty: her wonderful job and the fat salary it paid her. And Tom. Worst of all, she would lose Tom.

Shelly slid the check free of the paperclip. She wanted to tear it to bits. The need to destroy it was so powerful, her hand shook. But she made herself set it aside. Its existence might be useful, once she figured out exactly what she was going to do about this situation. She pinched open the brads that held the envelope's flap and folded it back so she could slide the envelope's contents out onto the desktop.

Photocopied clippings. A pile of them. Just as her uncle had promised. They told the story of Tom's crime and punishment. Tom had worked for Drake and Drake had used him and then discarded him, sacrificed him to save himself. No, the clippings didn't say that. They were merely articles about Tom's arrest and conviction. Shelly put the pieces together and came up with the truth behind the headlines.

The last clipping told of Tom's sentence for insider trading. There was a pink sticky note attached to it. Four letters and two numbers, S4CR4T, were written neatly on the pink note: the password.

Shelly put everything, in order, back in the envelope, leaving the sticky note where she'd found it. She paper-clipped the check back in place.

Now what?

This wasn't the kind of thing she would discuss on the phone, so calling Tom right now and laying it on him wasn't an option.

Get someone to watch Max and go to Tom? Her uncle had said he'd had her followed. He knew of the times she'd been to Tom's apartment. She wouldn't put it past Drake to have someone waiting outside, assigned to follow her if she left the house tonight.

Would it matter if Drake found out she'd run to Tom? Would it matter if he realized that she wasn't bought and paid for, after all?

She had no idea—yet it did seem wiser not to tip her hand. And that meant she'd have to wait until tomorrow, at work, to tell Tom what she knew.

The night was going to be a long one. Shelly set herself the task of enduring it.

The next morning, Tom arrived at the office feeling confident that he and Helen and the team of company lawyers and investigators had done all they could to plug the leak created by D'Amitri's indiscretion and the clever thievery of Lillian Todd.

Tom suspected that the Todd woman belonged to Thatcher, though TAKA-Hanson's investigators had yet to dig up proof that was so. Tom knew Thatcher's methods. Drake liked to infiltrate the competition, work from the inside to mess things around. Chances were he had others placed within the company, screwing up the works wherever they saw the chance, keeping Thatcher in the loop as to TAKA-Hanson's next move.

The job now was to find out who those others were.

Shelly was there, at her desk, as always, well ahead of him. He warmed inside at the sight of her. The last few days had been hectic. He hadn't had a spare moment to spend with her.

And damn, he had missed her. Maybe this afternoon, they could escape for an hour or two, share a little time alone before she left to pick up Max from daycare.

She watched him come toward her, those brown eyes wide, her expression…what? Apprehensive? Afraid?

She rose. "Got a minute?"

"For you? Always." He gestured her ahead of him into his office.

"Shut the door, please," she said, once they were both inside. She turned and he saw she had a large envelope in her hand.

He shut the door and tried a smile. "Hey." He tried teasing her. "If you want to jump my bones, I can spare half an hour. But make it quick."

She backed up a step and then drew herself up tall.

"I...don't think you'll be wanting to make love with me after you hear what I have to say."

He wasn't getting it. "Winston. What the hell?"

She gestured with the envelope. "Would you just... sit down?"

He shrugged. "Sure." And he went around behind his desk and dropped into his chair. "Okay. I'm sitting. What next?"

She took the chair opposite him, setting the envelope carefully in her lap. "I...I don't know where to start."

"Shelly. You're freaking me out here."

"I'm sorry, I... It's about Drake Thatcher."

Chapter Eleven

Tom's heart froze dead in his chest. "What did you say?"

He watched her swallow. Hard. Her cheeks were deadly pale and there was a rim of paleness around her soft lips. "Drake Thatcher is my uncle, my mother's half brother. I had never met him in my life until a month ago. The branches of the family, they…don't keep in touch much. But out of nowhere, he called me. That was on Monday the ninth of June. He took me out to dinner and when I told him I was looking for a job, he told me there would be something coming up at TAKA-Hanson and I should apply the next day. I did."

She fell silent. And then she just sat there, looking at him. He knew she expected him to respond. But he couldn't speak. He was too busy wondering if this could really be happening.

"Tom. Please. Say something...."

He gave her what she wanted, his voice as cold as the sudden ice that had formed around his heart. "You're one of Thatcher's people. Is that what you're telling me, that you're one of Thatcher's spies?"

She gasped and put her hand to her throat. "No," she whispered. "He planned for me to be, but I'm not."

"Then why the hell haven't you mentioned him before? Why is this the first time I've ever heard that bastard's name from your lips?"

"Tom. Please..." She reached toward him.

He looked at her outstretched fingers in disgust. "Answer me."

She drew her hand back, let it fall to her lap. "I was afraid, okay? I was...a coward. He told me that he had 'enemies' at TAKA-Hanson and if I used his name I would never be hired. I needed this job. I needed it bad—and I wanted it even more than I needed it. So I didn't mention him. I kept my mouth shut. It was dishonest of me. I know that. But I never... All I did was come to work here and do the best job that I could. All I did was..." She looked away. Whatever she was going to say next, she held it back.

They sat there facing each other, in a silence as deep as the grave.

So. He'd been had. Again. Drake's own damn niece. He could almost laugh about it. Really, it was funny as hell. Taken again. This time by a pair of wide brown eyes and an open, honest smile.

Honest. Right.

She turned the envelope over and he saw there was a check clipped to it. She slid it across the desk toward him. "Last night, Drake finally, um, called in his marker on me, I guess you could say. He gave me that check and that envelope. He told me for the first time that he…knew you personally, that you had once worked for him, that you hated him and if you ever knew I was related to him, that he had told me about this job, you would hate me, too."

Tom said nothing. He set the check aside, opened the envelope and spilled out the contents onto his desk.

"He gave me those clippings," she said, "for proof of his story about you. He gave me those and he gave me that password you see on the pink note. He said it was still good, and that I should use it right away, to get into the system and find out where else you would be opening The Taka hotels beyond San Francisco and Kyoto. He wanted to know what builders you had approached, what suppliers you had lined up. He said he needed to get going on getting 'his people' in place. He also said…" Her voice trailed off. She reached up, laid her hand against her forehead. "Oh, God…"

"Say it," he commanded. "Say the rest."

"Yes." She lowered her hand, squared her shoulders. "I know. I am. He said…that 'decisions had been made' to get rid of you, that what's in that envelope, the details of what happened fourteen years ago, would be leaked to the press and that you would be asked to leave TAKA-Hanson."

Tom swore. "When? When will the press get this?"

"He didn't say, other than that it would be right away. Today or tomorrow, I think. He told me to get into the computer system here immediately, this morning, and copy the information he wanted. When I had it, I was supposed to call him at a number he gave me last month, to leave a message on his voice mail. He said he'd be in touch to tell me what to do next. He said when you were asked to leave, I'd be leaving, too, and he wanted to make use of me before that happened. I...I tried to get him to admit that Lil Todd was working for him, but he laughed and said he didn't know anyone by that name."

Tom picked up the phone and dialed Helen's cell. When she answered, he said, "Get Jack. And Mori, if he's available. We've got a problem and we need to get on it fast."

While he waited for the others to arrive for the meeting, Tom did some checking into Shelly's story. He also kept her in his office, sitting in the chair across from his desk, where he could watch her every move.

She didn't say a word the whole time. Her silent presence reproached him, and that made him even more furious at her than he already was.

An hour after Tom called the meeting, they assembled in one of the top-floor meeting rooms.

Jack Hanson, the oldest of Helen's stepsons by her first husband, showed up several minutes after Helen and Mori. Jack had his own successful legal career separate from the company. But he was very much a member of the family and on call to provide legal counsel whenever any branch of TAKA-Hanson required his services.

Once he got there, they all took seats around the room's oval central table.

Tom took charge. He turned to Shelly, who waited, white-faced and silent, her hands folded in her lap.

"Tell them," he said. "Everything that you told me."

She repeated her story in a soft, clear voice, her gaze locked on the door that led out to the hallway, her expression tense and desperate—as if she longed to leap up and run for that door, to fling it wide and flee the room, the building, the whole ugly mess she had made.

Not a chance, Tom thought. Shelly Winston wasn't going anywhere. Not until he was damn good and ready to let her go.

When she finished telling her story, they questioned her about what she'd told them. She answered carefully, precisely, repeating her story until it became painfully clear that she'd told all she knew.

"Enough?" Tom asked, when there was silence. "Take a moment. Be sure. Once we have her escorted out of here, chances are she'll disappear."

Shelly spoke up then, her voice stronger than before—determined. And firm. "I have no intention of disappearing anywhere. If there's anything else I can do, simply give me a call. Also, if there's any advantage to you in having my uncle think I'm still going to do what he asked me to do, maybe it would work out better if I didn't change my routine. If one of your security guards escorts me from the building, it's more than likely that Drake Thatcher will know. He said he's had me followed, so I'm guessing that now, when it really matters, he's going to have someone watching me."

Tom grunted. "There's no way to tell what he knows right now. He could still have spies in the building, taking notes on the fact that we're in this meeting."

Shelly shook her head. "I'm sorry. If he had someone else in the building reporting to him, why ask an unknown quantity like me to get him the information he wants?"

Tom sent her a dismissive glance. "You *say* you're an unknown quantity to Thatcher. But we have no way of knowing if that's true."

Shelly looked down at her folded hands. "If you choose not to believe me, well, I completely understand."

Helen said gently, "I think Shelly's point is well taken. And, Shelly, I'm getting the impression you do want to help us any way you can. Is that right?"

"Yes. I do."

Tom wanted to call her a liar, to shout her down right then and there. He wanted to hurt her—for her betrayal of his trust, for his own idiocy in giving that trust in the first place. But he kept quiet. If Helen wanted to take the lead here, so much the better. Cooler heads should prevail—and right then, he was anything but cool.

"We would like to trust you," Helen said quietly, "but I'm sure you can see that wouldn't be in our best interests right now. However, if you honestly want to help, you can allow Tom to escort you to his office. Someone from security will join you there and wait with you until we come to some kind of decision as to what to do next."

Shelly stood. "That would be fine with me."

Tom cast a questioning glance at Helen. Shelly was as good as fired, and when an employee was fired, security accompanied them everywhere—including to the door.

Helen read his look, "I think a security guard leading her to the other end of the floor would attract attention we don't need right now."

"I see your point." He nodded at his colleagues and spoke to Shelly without actually looking at her. "Let's go, then."

She followed him back to his office. Another secretary, an emergency replacement sent up by HR to handle phone calls, sat at her desk. The woman smiled at them as they went by.

The guard tapped on Tom's door a few minutes after he and Shelly entered. Tom let him in and spoke to Shelly for the first time since they'd left the others in the meeting room.

"It doesn't make a whole lot of sense for you to stay if you call Thatcher the minute I leave the room."

Without a word, she fished her cell from her purse and handed it to the guard. Tom left her there, under guard, and rejoined the three in the meeting room.

He told them, "I had an hour or so to kill before you got here. I put the time to use gathering what information I could on this. Also, you should know that I've already had a call from a reporter at the *Tribune*. He left a message requesting I get back to him right away to confirm or deny a story they've just received."

Helen sighed. "You're saying that what Shelly just told us checks out?"

"That's what it looks like." Tom gathered the clippings from the table and put them back in the envelope. "As to the password…" He tapped the envelope for emphasis. "It belongs to one of my managers—Jessica Valdez."

Helen made a low sound of distress. "I can't believe that Jessica's working for Thatcher."

"Neither can I. And if she were, why give the password to Thatcher? Why not just copy the files herself?"

They called Jessica in and told her that someone had tried using her password to hack into the TAKA-Hanson computer system.

Jessica seemed honestly stunned. She swore she'd never shared her password with anyone. They told her to change it and sent her back to her desk.

Once she was gone, Tom vouched for her. "She worked closely with Louie on more than one project. And just recently, Jessica has been between secretaries. Lillian Todd stepped in and helped her out. I'd guess what happened is the Todd woman got lucky at some point and saw Jessica enter her password."

Helen frowned. "So you believe Lil Todd was working for Thatcher?"

Tom shrugged. "It's just a possible explanation—I have no proof."

"It makes sense, though," said Jack. "And anyway, you can't reassign everyone in the hospitality division. I suggest you limit Jessica's access to nonsensitive information for the time being and keep an eye on her."

Mori and Helen agreed.

Tom tried to look on the bright side. "Maybe we'll

get lucky and Jessica's password will be the last leak we need to plug."

"From what I'm learning about this Thatcher character, I wouldn't count on that," said Jack wryly.

"Don't worry, I'm counting on nothing. And as far as the coming media storm over my checkered past, I think there's only one sensible solution. I'm resigning, as of today."

"No," said Jack.

"A bad idea," said Mori.

Helen said, "Absolutely not."

"Come on," Tom told them all wearily. "It's the only way."

Helen wasn't having any of that. "There's never only one way. We knew this could happen two years ago. I hired you then and I'd do it again. You've exceeded our expectations of you right down the line."

Tom rubbed the back of his neck, trying to ease out a little of the tension. "Yeah, well. The point is it *has* happened, and the company doesn't need this kind of trouble. I go, you do damage control when it all hits the fan, and TAKA-Hanson comes out of it strong as ever."

Jack was watching his stepmother. "I know that look. Helen's got a plan."

"Of course I've got a plan. And a good one, too."

The plan depended on the Hanson North America arm of the company, which was media. Print, radio and television were all going to be put to use starting immediately. Jack enlisted his wife, Samantha, a Hanson N.A. vice president who had contacts in every corner of the media community, to make the calls and set up the series of radio and TV spots. The hope was to scoop Thatcher on the story, to get their version on the street ahead of his.

But even if Thatcher's story came out first, Helen's and Tom's interviews would serve as a powerful rebuttal—or so they hoped.

Helen and Tom did the print interviews together via conference call that afternoon. Tom called his contacts at the industry rags. They were only too happy to hear Tom's story, told by Helen.

It was the tale of an ambitious young man from a poor, hardworking family, a young man who went too far and broke the law. Helen explained how the young man was tried and convicted and paid his debt to society. How he'd worked for over a decade to turn his life around. And how he'd succeeded.

"Readers will lap this up," said the reporter from the *Tribune*. "You're a damn hero, Tom. A true American success story."

"It's a good title," said Helen. "'An American Success Story.' Be sure to write how proud we are at TAKA-Hanson to have Tom on our team."

The reporter promised he would write just that.

By the end of the day, Samantha had Helen and Tom lined up for Chicago's top TV morning show on Channel 9 and a series of drive-time interviews at three major radio stations the next day.

Jack reported, "Samantha says her work here is done."

Helen said, "Tom. Before you take off, I need a few minutes...."

"About?"

"Shelly."

It was quarter to five when Tom returned to his office. He found Shelly sitting patiently on the couch and the guard standing at the window looking out over the Magnificent Mile.

He told the guard to give Shelly back her phone and then let him go.

Once Tom was alone with the woman he'd so stupidly trusted, he said, "By tomorrow morning, Thatcher will know that you blew the whistle on him."

She tipped her soft chin high and met his eyes. "Fine with me. Does this mean I can go and pick up my son now?"

He didn't answer her. Instead, he said flatly, "I can understand, objectively, why you did what you did."

Softly she added, "But you can't forgive me."

He thought about kissing her, about the soft resilience of her body beneath his hands, of the scent of her that pleased him so deeply, a scent that seemed, somehow, made just for him.

He glanced away from her. Bad idea, to think about the smell of her or the feel of her lips under his. "I can't…I can't have you working for me anymore."

"Tom." She was waiting, he knew, for him to look at her.

He made himself do it, though it tore something within him to gaze into those brandy-brown eyes again.

She said, "I didn't know about you and Thatcher. He never told me until last night. And neither did you."

Gruffly, he demanded, "And that makes it okay, that you never happened to mention how you came to apply for Verna's job? That makes it okay that you lied to me in the interview, that first day we met, that you told me how you'd heard 'good things' about TAKA-Hanson, how you just happened to 'drop in' to get your résumé on file?"

"No. It doesn't make it okay. I was afraid to lose a job I needed and wanted so badly, so I lied and I withheld important information. But, Tom, come on. So did you. You never told me about what my uncle did to you, about the price you paid. About your parents. That was what you meant, wasn't it? When you said you *hadn't* made them proud? For some reason, you could tell me about the child you lost. But you couldn't tell me about—"

"Stop." He put up a hand to silence her. "I don't want to hear it. I shouldn't have told you anything. I realize that now."

"Oh, Tom…"

"Don't look at me like that." He turned from her and went to the window and stared blindly down at the traffic crawling by all those stories below. "I spoke with Helen. What you told us today *was* invaluable to TAKA-Hanson and to The Taka hotel project. It's clear to everyone that you never betrayed this company and you never *would* have betrayed TAKA-Hanson, that in the crunch, you more than did your part. You will be paid a large bonus. And, since Helen insists that you deserve a second chance, HR will place you in another division. Media, maybe. Or software. You'll receive a check for the bonus within the week and HR should be calling you soon to offer you a new position."

She said nothing.

He turned on her. "What? Is that unacceptable to you?"

"Oh, please. Of course it's acceptable. It's...very generous. More than I ever would have expected."

"Helen's a hell of a woman."

"Yeah. She is."

"Come here."

She drew in a slow, shuddering breath. "Oh, God. Tom, don't..."

"Come here. Now." Something dark and a little twisted within him took harsh pleasure in tormenting her, in mocking the intimacy they had once shared— right here, in this room.

She approached him slowly. He despised himself for admiring the easy sway of her hips, the curve of her waist, the roundness of her breasts beneath the pretty yellow dress she wore. At the edge of his desk, she hesitated.

"Don't stop there." He crooked a finger, a gesture that once would have teased her, but in this situation was nothing short of purposely cruel.

She shook her head, bit her lip. But still, she took another step. And another after that. Until she stood before him in front of the wide window, close enough that he could see the flecks of gold in her brown eyes, the misty sheen to them that spoke of tears she refused to shed. Close enough that he could breathe in the sweet, fresh scent of her.

She swallowed, hard. "All right. I'm here. What do you want?"

"Give me your hand."

She hesitated, but she did it. She laid that soft, cool hand of hers in his. He imagined allowing himself to give a sharp tug, to pull her sweet body up hard against him. He saw himself bringing his mouth down on hers, sucking all that sweetness into himself, stripping off the yellow dress and anything she had beneath it, laying her across his desk and entering her.

Taking her. Having her.

One more time.

He did no such thing. Instead, he took Thatcher's check from his pocket and laid it in her palm. With slow care, he closed her fingers around it. "This is yours. I'd cash it fast. By tomorrow, there's bound to be a stop payment on it."

She stepped back from him, her face deadly pale, except for two bright flags of color high on her cheeks. "If I intended to cash it, I wouldn't have turned it over to you."

He slanted her a dismissing look. "Hey. Fifty thousand dollars is a nice wad of cash. Why not keep it? You certainly earned it."

She held up the check to him. "Watch." And then, with slow deliberation, she tore it in two, and in two again. She let the pieces drift to the floor between them.

"Noble," he said.

She only stared at him, eyes flashing with defiance and fury—and hurt. "I'll ask you again. May I go now?"

"One more thing."

"Say it. Get it over with."

"I want to meet with Thatcher. I want you to help me make that happen."

She shook her head. "You don't get it."

"Get what?"

"It's not as if I dial a number and he answers. I call him. And then, maybe, he calls me back. Eventually. Or maybe he just shows up at the curb in front of my house in a limousine. He takes his time about getting back to me. I'm…a low priority with him, to put it mildly. If, as you've predicted, by tomorrow he knows I'm not on his side, I doubt I'll ever see him again. I have no idea what makes you think I could even get him to call me, let alone get him to meet with you. You'd have more luck just calling him yourself."

"All right," he said after a moment. "What you say makes sense."

"Great. May I go?"

"You said you have a number for him."

"That's right."

"Give me the number. Then you can go."

For a long, slow moment, she regarded him. He wasn't sure what he saw in those eyes. He only knew it was going to take him a long time to get over her.

But he would.

Tom Holloway was a survivor. He knew how to move on. He'd done it often enough, each time leaving pieces of himself behind. But he was still standing, still moving forward, still determined that nothing—not even sweet Shelly Winston's betrayal—would hold him back for long.

She got out her cell and flipped it open and punched a couple of buttons. Then she went to his desk, took a pen from the pencil drawer and scribbled a number on his desk pad. "Knock yourself out." She flipped the phone shut and headed for the door.

He stayed where he was, by the window, unmoving, until she was gone.

Chapter Twelve

Shelly held it together through the train ride to Max's daycare. She put a resolute smile on her face and exchanged small talk with one of the teachers while he gathered his things from his cubby.

They got back on the train to ride the rest of the way home. The car they ended up on was packed, as usual. They held the rail and the train sped toward their stop. Halfway there, Max tugged on her arm.

"Hmm? What, honey?"

"Are you sick, Mom? You don't look so good."

"I'm fine." She stared past the blank faces of their fellow passengers, out the smeared windows, seeing nothing, trying not to remember the hurtful things Tom had said to her.

"Mom?"

"What?"

"You're not really fine, are you?"

She made herself look down at him, made herself give him a reassuring smile. "I've got a lot on my mind, that's all."

He studied her face. "Oh," he said at last in a small voice. "You mean you're not going to tell me, right?"

"I'm fine. Really," she said again.

And her little boy shrugged and let it go.

At home, she let him watch the television while she put a salad together and broiled a pair of chicken breasts. When the food was ready, she had him set up trays and they ate in front of the TV.

As a rule, Shelly insisted on real family dinners, where they sat at the two-seater table in the kitchen and shared conversation instead of staring at a television screen. Tonight, she was grateful for something to stare at, for the bright colors of the cartoons Max enjoyed, for the music and the sound of recorded voices. She knew she wouldn't have made it through the meal without breaking down if she had to look at her son's sweet, open face behind his new glasses and know that *he* knew something wasn't right, though he didn't understand what that something could be.

After the meal, she shooed him into his room to play on his own for a while. At eight, he had his bath. And at eight-thirty, she tucked him in.

He folded his arms on top of the sheet. "I was thinking that I should prob'ly call Tom tonight."

Tears scalded the back of her throat. She swallowed

them down. She would have to tell him something, about Tom. Just, please, not tonight.

"You called him last night," she reminded him in a voice so bright and brittle it seemed it might crack.

Last night, before Drake showed up. When Tom still trusted me.

Max tried again. "I think he likes for me to call him."

"Not tonight."

"Mom…"

"Not tonight." She pecked his cheek and stood, swiftly, turning to shut the curtains and get out of there before he could ask her again.

She was lucky. He gave it up. She escaped into the hall and shut his door and leaned against it, trembling.

It could have been worse, she reminded herself. Yes, she'd lost Tom. But she hadn't disgraced herself— except in his eyes.

Helen still trusted her. Soon, she would have another job, a job as good as the one with Tom had been.

Everything would be okay. She didn't have to pound the pavement, hoping against hope that something would turn up.

It could have been worse.

She had to remember that.

She had to…

The tears spilled over. She cried, silently, standing there in the hall at her son's bedroom door, the hopeless sobs shaking her frame, but no sound escaping her.

Finally, when the tears slowed a little, she went to her own room, shut the door and called her mother.

Norma answered on the second ring.

Shelly said, "Hi, Mom."

Norma knew her too well. "Oh, honey. You sound so strange. What's happened?"

The concern in her mom's voice brought a fresh flood of tears. "Oh, Mom. Mom, I…"

"What? Tell me. It's okay. You can tell me."

It was all the encouragement Shelly needed. Between sobs and honks into a boxfull of tissues, she told her mother everything.

At the end, Norma said, "That bastard Drake. I should have known he'd pull some crap like this."

Shelly gasped to hear her sweet mother use such strong language. "Mom!"

"What? Well, I'm sorry. I have a mind to give him a call and tell him exactly what I think of him."

"Don't. Please. He's so not worth it—not to mention that he never answers his phone."

"You're right, of course. But still. It would be so satisfying to call him a bad name or two right to his face."

"It's not necessary."

"Do you realize that that man has had *five* wives? I hope every one of them took him to the cleaners when they divorced him."

Shelly laughed. "I love you, Mom."

"I love you, too. So very much. And I know you and Tom will work it out. Sometimes, it seems impossible, but when there's love—"

"Mom. Stop."

"But, honey—"

"It's over between Tom and me. What we had, it's…broken now, beyond repair. He won't forgive me for not telling him about Drake—for even being *related* to the man."

"Give it time."

"Time won't do it. It's over. I mean it. I…" The tears started in again. She tried to gulp them back.

"Come home," Norma said.

"I… Oh, I don't think—"

"Rent a car tomorrow morning. Or fly to St. Louis and we'll pick you up. I mean it. You need your family around you right now. You and Max come home for a few days. You let us take care of you. You do what I say."

Shelly gulped down more pointless tears and opened her mouth to protest some more. But then she realized that home was exactly where she needed to be.

"Okay. We'll come."

"There you go. That's what I wanted to hear."

Once all the excitement was over for the day, Tom had a pile of catch-up work to do. He didn't get back to his place until after nine.

He called the number Shelly had given him and left a message for Drake. Then he poured himself two fingers of good Scotch and stood looking out at the small sliver of Lake Michigan he could see from his dining room window, trying not to think about Shelly.

The phone rang when he was halfway through his drink.

Tom picked it up. Before he said a word, Drake spoke. "I'm guessing this means my niece has told all. So discouraging. A man can't even count on his own family these days."

Tom knocked back the rest of his drink and relished the burn as it slid down his throat. "Are you in town?"

"I could be."

Tom named a bar a few blocks from his apartment. "Ten-thirty," he said and hung up.

At the bar, he took a corner table, ordered a drink and let it sit in front of him, untouched.

Drake arrived at ten-forty. He slid into the chair opposite Tom and ordered Maker's Mark on the rocks. They both waited until the waitress had served him and left them alone.

Like Tom, Drake didn't so much as glance at his drink. He said, "You're looking well."

Tom quelled the urge to punch Thatcher's lights out and reminded himself once again that Drake wasn't worth beating up. He was your common, everyday, run-of-the-mill antisocial personality. The power and the thrill of besting other people was his greatest pleasure in life. Tom had known this about him from the first—and had become his protégé anyway. Back then, Tom had imagined he could handle Drake.

He'd been paying the price for such a serious miscalculation ever since.

"You've been making trouble for me again," Tom said.

"Nothing personal," Drake lied. It was always personal between Drake and Tom. Tom had survived what Drake had tried to do to him—repeatedly. Every time Drake knocked him down, Tom got back up again.

Tom reminded himself that getting back up again was the best revenge, the only revenge that mattered. He wondered why he didn't feel better about it.

Because the price is too damn high.

It came to him then. The price. This time the price was Shelly.

He saw then, as he stared into Drake's black, bottomless eyes, that he had lost again—just when he thought he'd won.

For the first time, he didn't have to start over. He'd triumphed over Thatcher and kept his job—while losing what mattered most: Shelly. Max. The impossible dream that never came true, the fading hope for love and a family at last...

Tom realized with horror that though Drake would never know it, he *had* won again.

Thatcher smiled. "So, once more, the past has caught up with you. You seem very calm this time."

"I think I've gotten used to this. It always ends up here, somehow, doesn't it?"

"Tomorrow," Drake said with great satisfaction, "the story will break. You'll be out of a job again. I wish I could say I was sorry about that."

Tom corrected him. "No, you don't."

Drake shrugged. "You should give up, you know. I'll never allow you to climb too high. I can't afford that. You might become a danger to me. And that can never happen."

Tom let him gloat. It was the point of this meeting. Let the SOB get all full of himself—only to find out tomorrow that Helen Taka-Hanson was way ahead of him, smarter and quicker. Helen hadn't fallen for Thatcher's tricks.

Tom picked up his drink and sipped it. Slowly. He

was supposed to be feeling triumphant about now, relishing his victory while Drake imagined that *he* was the winner tonight.

But Tom didn't feel triumphant. He felt…empty. Bested. Trumped.

Drake stood. "Great to see you, Tom. Nice to share this time together."

Tom nodded. He watched the other man walk away, marveling. He had won the game this time.

And lost what really mattered. Again.

And again, it was his own damn fault.

"But, Mom. I have to go to daycare today. I can't go to Granny's. I've already *been* to Granny's."

Shelly, at the sink cleaning up after breakfast, glanced over her shoulder. Max stood in the middle of the kitchen floor. Though Shelly had told him fifteen minutes ago that he needed to get dressed, he still wore his pajamas.

The best-behaved kid in Chicago—and he chose *today* to give her grief.

She grabbed a towel. Wiping her hands, she turned to him. "You love to go to Granny's. And we're only staying for a little while. You'll be back in daycare before you know it."

"What if the butterflies hatch before I get back? What about my Popsicle-stick fort that I haven't finished making yet?"

"I'm sorry, Max. We're going. Now get dressed, please."

"But what about Tom?"

Shelly tried not to gape. Kids. They always somehow seemed to know way more than you thought they did. Shelly tossed the towel to the counter behind her and knelt to face her son eye-to-eye.

He reached out, laid his small hand on her shoulder. "You were crying last night, Mom. I heard you."

Oh, God. Tears clogged her throat all over again. She gulped them down.

Truth, she thought. The simple truth. Always the best way. After what had happened with Tom, she would never again let herself forget that lies brought nothing but trouble and an eventual bleak day of reckoning.

She said, "We, um, we won't be seeing Tom anymore. And I won't be working for him. When we get back from Granny's, I'm going to start a new job."

"But doesn't Tom need you? To type and stuff like that?"

"Tom will get another assistant."

"But...you like Tom. Tom likes you. *I* like Tom."

"Sometimes things don't work out."

"Why not?"

Why not? Dangerous question. "I can't explain any more right now. We have to go. We need to get to the airport."

"If you just called him—or I could call him. I could tell him that he needs to—"

"Max." She rose.

He was silent, looking up at her.

"We are going to Granny's. Get dressed. Now."

His small chin quivered and his mouth formed a straight line. She was absolutely certain that her reasonable, well-behaved son was about to throw a full-blown temper tantrum.

But then he said, "Okay." And he turned and left the kitchen.

Shelly watched him go, a terrible hollowness in her stomach and a weakness in her knees. It was her worst fear realized. Not only did *she* have to get over Tom.

Her son would have to, as well.

Max knew the rules about calling people. He knew very well that you had to ask first and you were not allowed to be a pest.

But when he left his mom in the kitchen, he didn't know what else to do. Things were not good and he wanted to make them all right again.

So he broke the rules, just that one time.

He tiptoed into his mom's room and he picked up the phone by her bed and he dialed Tom's cell number.

Tom and Helen knocked some serious socks off in the Channel 9 interview.

Helen was amazing—cool and confident as ever. Honest and direct. She told the pretty cohost how she'd hired Tom with the full knowledge that he'd once gone to prison. That she'd never regretted giving Tom another chance.

Tom played back-up to Helen's starring role. He was low-key and modest. He answered the cohost's questions in a simple, understated way. He was humble. And he was grateful to have another chance. And to be working for a dynamic, creative company like TAKA-Hanson.

When the interview was over, both hosts shook their hands and the producer fell all over them. "Dynamite," he said. "Great job, both of you...."

They left the studio and ducked into a car that took them to one drive-time radio spot after another. Each one went better than the last.

It was after eleven when they got back to the office. Jack, Samantha and Mori were waiting in one of the conference rooms with several copies each of the *Tribune* and the *Daily News,* both of which had run the story Drake gave them side-by-side with the rebuttal Tom and Helen had provided.

"Congratulations," said Samantha warmly.

"Slam dunk," added Jack.

Mori smiled and nodded his approval in that regal, reserved way he had.

Tom got back to his own office at a little after noon. He had his temporary secretary bring him lunch at his desk and he worked the rest of the afternoon to get back on top of the job after a day and a half spent fixing what Drake Thatcher had tried to break.

Drake called him on the office line at two. He didn't bother to say hello. "It appears I've underestimated the situation this time around. Don't worry, though. I'll regroup."

"Is that a threat?"

"Whatever gave you that idea? Tell me, what did you do with my niece? I really did hope to have a word with her, but some stranger answered the phone just now."

"Try Shelly at home."

"You've fired her, haven't you?" Thatcher spoke with relish.

"No. She's just taking a few days off." It was true, as far as it went. "Anything else?"

"Not a thing," said Drake. "I think we've said it all—for now." The line went dead.

At two that afternoon, Shelly stood by the window in an upstairs bedroom of her mother's house. The room had been Shelly's through all the years from childhood to the day she left for college. White sheers hung on the windows. They had wide ruffles along the edges and matching ruffled tie-backs. The sheers had hung there for as long as Shelly could remember. Behind the sheers, for privacy, there were old-fashioned roll-down shades.

She heard the back porch screen creak shut and watched her dad and her son cross the wide swathe of green lawn, headed for the trees that rimmed the creek. Shelly smiled to herself. Maybe Max would find his pollywog, all grown-up into a frog.

Her cell chimed from her purse on the low dresser by the door.

Tom? In spite of everything he'd said and done, her heart lifted in bright, impossible hope.

She hustled over there and got the phone from her bag. The display shouted a number she didn't recognize.

Fine, she tried to tell herself. She didn't want to talk to Tom, anyway. Never. Never again.

"Hello?"

Her uncle said, "Shelly."

She almost hung up on him. But then she sighed. "What?"

"You've disappointed me. I thought I should let you know I've put a stop on that check."

"Fine with me. I don't want your money. I want nothing to do with you. Ever again."

He actually clucked his tongue at her. "I must remember in the future not to hand out career opportunities to poor relations." Her mom appeared in the open doorway a few feet from where she stood.

She spoke to her uncle one last time. "Good. Never call me again." She snapped the phone firmly shut.

Norma said, "Let me guess. Drake?"

Shelly dropped the phone back into her purse. "What a horrible man."

Norma shrugged. "I never did really understand that side of the family." She looked at Shelly so fondly and Shelly thought how fortunate she was, to have been born to loving parents. "It's good," her mom said, "to have you home."

Shelly sat on the edge of the bed. Norma sat close beside her, wrapping a comforting arm around Shelly's shoulder.

"I saw this morning's *Tribune*," Norma said.

"Yes," Shelly answered softly. "It worked out well for Tom, don't you think?"

"Very well."

Shelly said, "I'm glad that Tom will keep his job, that Drake didn't succeed in messing him over again."

They were quiet for a moment. Then her mom said, "If you need to cry…"

Shelly chuckled. "You know, I think I'm pretty much all cried out. For the time being, anyway."

"We'll have pot roast for dinner."

"I'm hungry just thinking about it."

"However things end up," said her mother, "love is never wrong."

"I never said it was love, Mom, between Tom and me."

"Oh, honey. You didn't have to."

Tom didn't get home that night until after eight. And he didn't get around to checking his cell-phone voice mail until he was getting ready for bed and realized he'd left the phone off the whole day.

There were three messages that could wait until tomorrow.

The fourth felled him like a punch to the gut. He sank to the edge of the bed when he heard the little boy's voice.

"Tom, it's Max Winston. I know I'm not s'posed to call unless I ask first. But you made my mom cry. Now we're going to Granny's even though I haven't finished my fort yet. In case you want to come and say you're sorry, my Granny lives at 321 Cherry Vale in Mount Vernon. I think you should come, Tom. You should come right away."

Chapter Thirteen

The next morning, Shelly rose early. She went down into the kitchen where her mother, in old jeans and a worn yellow T-shirt with the words The Jimi Hendrix Experience in psychedelic purple across the front, was already busy frying bacon at the stove.

She turned and gave Shelly one of her biggest, happiest smiles. "While you're home, I'll do my best to harden up those arteries."

"Smells great. What can I do to help?"

"Not a thing. Let me spoil you. Have some coffee. Go sit on the porch and enjoy the beautiful summer morning."

"Want me to feed the chickens?"

"Max is handling that."

"Well, okay." Shelly went to the coffeemaker and filled one of her mom's orange mugs. "Call me when it's time to eat." She wandered out through the central hall. The heavy oak front door stood open. She pushed the storm door wide enough to slip through to the porch.

The house, like all the houses on Cherry Vale, was set back from the street, with a winding gravel driveway leading up to the front porch and then curving away toward the detached two-car garage. Shelly sat on the front steps, elbows braced on her knees, and sipped her coffee, enjoying the pleasant warmth of the summer morning, and the soft, sighing sound the trees made as the wind rustled through them. She watched a cardinal, impossibly red, as it flitted across the driveway and vanished into the trees.

She heard a blue jay squawking somewhere over near the garage and turned toward the sound.

The crunch of tires on gravel surprised her. She looked back to see a silver Cadillac rolling toward her.

Tom was behind the wheel.

The shock was so powerful, she almost let her coffee cup slip from her hands. Some of the hot brew still got away from her and scalded her fingers.

She wished a hundred things at once: that she'd worn something more pulled-together than old cutoffs, flip-flops and a wrinkled camp shirt; that her heart would stop racing; that the stupid tears of surprise and infuriating hope wouldn't rise…

Somehow, she made herself stand. She set her cup on one of the two low brick pillars at the base of the porch steps.

And she waited for him to stop the damn car and get

out. When he did, she saw that he wore jeans and a dark blue polo shirt. He came right for her.

Shelly waited for him. She could do nothing else. She felt rooted to the spot at the base of the steps. He stopped a few feet from her. She saw the shadows under his blue eyes, and the worry.

And the pain.

She steeled herself against him, pulling her shoulders back, holding her head high. "What now?"

"Shelly…" He seemed not to know how to go on.

"How did you know I was here?"

"It doesn't matter."

Suddenly, she knew. "Max. Max called you."

"Shelly—"

She put up a hand. "It's no good."

"Don't say that."

"It's too late."

"No. No, it's not. I won't let it be."

"You can't…do this, Tom. It's not right. It's not fair."

"Just give me five minutes."

She was weakening already. God. She was such a wimp. "No."

And she whirled away from him. She raced up the steps, her flip-flops slapping hard against the old boards of the porch. Throwing back the storm door, she fled through the central hall, aware as she did it that running was silly, but somehow unable to stand there and let him see her tears.

Too bad he followed her. "Shelly. Damn it. Don't…" She heard his footfalls behind her, heard the storm door slam a second time.

"Go away." She threw the command back over her shoulder as she entered the kitchen.

Her mom was just setting the table. She looked up. "What the—?"

Max banged the back door wide as he came in from the rear porch. "Tom!" he cried. "You're here...."

Shelly ran on, through the door that Max had left open, across the back porch, out through the back screen, which didn't quite get a chance to slam before Tom was shoving it open again, pounding down the steps behind her.

The flip-flops hobbled her. So she kicked them away and took off across the grass, startling an old hen and her line of yellow chicks. The hen screeched and flapped her wings; the chicks cheeped wildly.

Shelly ran on, toward the birches that lined the creek. She reached them, ducking into their dappled shade and half sliding down the bank toward the clear, cool water.

At water's edge, she stopped. Slowly, she turned.

Tom had stopped, too, just beneath the canopy of the trees. "Five minutes," he said again.

Both of them were breathing hard.

And at least now she didn't feel as though she was going to lose it and start bawling like an idiot. Running like hell had somehow banished her tears.

She dropped to the bank, gathered her knees up close to her body and rested her chin on them.

There was silence, for a moment, just the sound of the water gurgling in the creek and the blue jays squawking and the gentle croak of a frog. Then she heard him coming toward her, fallen leaves crunching under his feet as he started down the bank.

He sat beside her. But he didn't try to touch her.

Which was good, she told herself. She didn't want him touching her.

"All right," she said, looking straight ahead at the opposite bank. "Since you refuse to go away, say whatever it is you came here to say. Just go ahead."

He didn't speak. Wasn't that just like a man? A woman said he could speak. And he didn't.

Unwillingly, she turned and looked at him.

Those blue eyes were waiting. He said, "I lost track of what matters. I've been battling Drake Thatcher for so many years, I started to think that winning the next skirmish with him was the goal. It wasn't. The goal was…a chance. To have a real life. A partnership with the right woman. A…family."

She gritted her teeth. "I hate this. You're making me want to cry again."

"Shelly. Please. I'm so damn sorry. You…you're what matters. You and Max. What we might make, together, over time."

"You…" She sniffed and gulped and willed the tears away. "You hurt me. What you did, in your office, when you handed me that check…that was cruel, Tom."

Shame darkened his eyes. "I know. It was unforgivable."

"And yet that's what you're here for, isn't it? To ask me to forgive you."

"That's right. I am—I realize I've got no right to expect your forgiveness. I *don't* expect it. But I want it.

More than anything, I want you to forgive me and maybe even try again with me."

"Forgive you," she repeated.

"Yes. Forgive me."

She shook her head, and then confessed, "I…was wrong, too. I know it. I should have told you everything, the day that you hired me. Or at least in Kyoto, on the night we first made love. But I didn't. I told myself that since I was never going to do anything to hurt you or TAKA-Hanson, there was no reason you had to know how I came to apply for the job as your assistant. I was…so afraid that the truth would cost me everything."

"You were right to be afraid. Look what happened when you did tell me."

She stared out at the creek again. "Yeah. It was all I'd feared, and worse."

"I should have been…better," he said. "A better man. I know it now. It's an old instinct in me, a powerful instinct. To fight and fight hard whenever Drake pops up again. It's not reasonable. It's not…fair. It's down and dirty and cruel. And I gave in to it, I turned it on you."

She said nothing. She dragged in a ragged breath and felt the need within herself to forgive him as he'd asked her to. To try again as he said he wanted. She wondered, *Is this love that I'm feeling? This pain that's so close to joy? This hope, this…rising sensation inside me?*

He said, "I met with Drake two nights ago in a bar not far from my apartment. I let him think he had won, all the while knowing that, the next morning, he'd be in for a big surprise. I expected to feel good, knowing I had bested him this time around. But all I thought of was how he'd won, after all. How I'd lost you, driven you away. And without you, my triumph was empty. Nothing. Less than that." He said her name, "Shelly?" Like a plea. Like a prayer.

"There will be honesty," she told him through the tears she fought to hold back. "Honesty between us. Always. I need to know that. I need to promise that. I need to hear you promise that to me."

He reached out. He touched the side of her face. She allowed that. He said, "Always."

"If it makes us nervous, if we're afraid to say it— then that's the very thing we have to tell each other. Do you promise me?"

"I promise. I do."

She whispered, "I believe you."

He took her shoulders. She allowed herself to sway toward him. Their lips met in a kiss that was awkward and searching and so very beautiful.

When he pulled away, his blue eyes shone. He said gruffly, "There's something already, a secret I need to tell you."

She realized she was holding her breath and made herself let it out in a rush. "Oh, God. What?"

"I love you," he said.

She stared. And then she laughed—a wild, happy laugh. There were tears on her cheeks. She swiped them away. "That's the secret? That you love me?"

"Shelly. It's huge. I love you. I've loved you for weeks now. Maybe since the night we sat on that bench outside the Newberry and you told me how you were never going to end up in my bed. Remember?"

"Oh, Tom. How could I ever forget?" She gulped. Hard.

"What?" he asked gently.

And she told him. "Tom. I love you, too."

And then he reached for her again. She went into his strong, cherishing arms. The kiss they shared then was better than any that had come before. It was tender and sweet and deep. It was a kiss to seal the most solemn of vows.

"Do you realize," he said, a few minutes later, "that if it wasn't for Drake Thatcher, we probably never would have met?"

She gazed at him with wonder. "It's true. How amazing."

"Come on." He stood and helped her to her feet.

They turned for her mother's house, together, hand in hand.

"What's that saying?" he asked her as they climbed the bank. "That living well is the best revenge..."

"Mmm-hmm." She turned a smile on him. "That's what they say."

"They're wrong." They emerged from the trees and started across the lawn.

"So, then what?" she asked and squeezed his hand.

"Not only living," he said. "Loving. Loving well. It's better than any revenge."

* * * * *

Don't miss the next chapter in the new
Special Edition continuity
BACK IN BUSINESS
Decorator-to-the-stars Ally Walker
returns to Chicago to take care of her mother and
finds herself trying—and failing—to resist
the charms of Dr. Jacob Fox.
Will this pair be a perfect match?

Look for
DESIGNS ON THE DOCTOR
by
Victoria Pade.
On sale August 2008,
wherever Silhouette books are sold.

Rufus, as Crystal Hayes had decided to call the black Lab, slept soundly on the soft seat even as she maneuvered the Softco truck in front of the Dean Grosso garage. Engines fired through the open bay doors, compressors clacked and impact tools whined as the teams tweaked their race cars in preparation for qualifying at the third race in Charlotte.

As always when she visited the garage area, Crystal experienced a vicarious thrill, watching the technicians' meticulous, last-minute preparations. As the daughter of a machinist, she understood the difference a fraction of a degree or a thousandth of an inch could make in the performance of a race car.

She muscled the driver's door shut behind her and

waved hello to a couple of familiar crew members in their white-and-pale-blue jump suits. Then she rounded the back of the truck and rolled up the door. Inside, five boxes were marked Cargill Motors.

One of them was big and heavy, and it had slid forward a few feet, probably when she'd braked to make the narrow parking lot entrance. So she pushed up the sleeves of her canary-yellow T-shirt, then stretched forward to reach the box. A couple of catcalls came her way as her faded blue jeans tightened across her rear end. But she knew they were good-natured, and she simply ignored them.

She dragged the box toward her over the gritty metal floor.

"Let me give you a hand with that," a deep, melodious voice rumbled in her ear.

"I can manage," she responded crisply, not wanting to engage with any of the catcallers.

Here in the garage, the last thing she needed was one of the guys treating her as if she was something other than, well, one of the guys.

She'd learned long ago there was something about her that made men toss out pickup lines like parade candy. And she'd been around race crews long enough to know she needed to behave like a buddy, not a potential date.

She piled the smaller boxes on top of the large one.

"It looks heavy," said the voice.

"I'm tough," she assured him as she scooped the pile into her arms.

He didn't move away, so she turned her head to

subject him to a *back off* stare. But she found herself staring into a compelling pair of green…no, brown… no, hazel eyes. She did a double take as they seemed to twinkle, multicolored, under the garage lights.

The man insistently held out his hands for the boxes. There was a dignity in his tone and little crinkles around his eyes that hinted at wisdom. There wasn't a single sign of flirtation in his expression, but Crystal was still cautious.

"You know I'm being paid to move this, right?" she asked him.

"That doesn't mean I can't be a gentleman."

Somebody whistled from a workbench. "Go, Professor Larry."

The man named Larry tossed a "Back off" over his shoulder. Then he turned to Crystal. "Sorry about that."

"Are you for real?" she asked, growing uncomfortable with the attention they were drawing. The last thing she needed was some latter-day Sir Galahad defending her honor at the track.

He quirked a dark eyebrow in a question.

"I mean," she elaborated, "you don't need to worry. I've been fending off the wolves since I was seventeen."

"Doesn't make it right," he countered, attempting to lift the boxes from her hands.

She jerked back. "You're not making it any easier."

He frowned.

"You carry this box, and they start thinking of me as a girl."

Professor Larry dipped his gaze to take in the curves

of her figure. "Hate to tell you this," he said, a little twinkle coming into those multifaceted eyes.

Something about his look made her shiver inside. It was a ridiculous reaction. Guys had given her the once-over a million times. She'd learned long ago to ignore it.

"Odds are," Larry continued, a teasing drawl in his tone, "they already have."

She turned pointedly away, boxes in hand as she marched across the floor. She could feel him watching her from behind.

* * * * *

*Crystal Hayes could do without her looks,
men obsessed with her looks and guys who think
they're God's gift to the ladies.
Would Larry be the one guy who could blow all
of Crystal's preconceptions away?
Look for OVERHEATED
by Barbara Dunlop.
On sale July 29, 2008.*

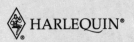

HARLEQUIN®

American ★ Romance®

MARIN THOMAS
A Coal Miner's Wife

HEARTS OF APPALACHIA

High-school dropout and recently widowed
Annie McKee has twin boys to raise. The
now single mom is torn between choosing
charity from her Appalachian clan or leaving
Heather's Hollow and finding a better future
for her boys. But her handsome neighbor and
deceased husband's best friend is determined
to show the proud widow there's nothing
secondhand about love!

**Available August
wherever books are sold.**

LOVE, HOME & HAPPINESS

REQUEST YOUR FREE BOOKS!

2 FREE NOVELS PLUS 2 FREE GIFTS!

SPECIAL EDITION®

Life, Love and Family!

YES! Please send me 2 FREE Silhouette Special Edition® novels and my 2 FREE gifts (gifts are worth about $10). After receiving them, if I don't wish to receive any more books, I can return the shipping statement marked "cancel." If I don't cancel, I will receive 6 brand-new novels every month and be billed just $4.24 per book in the U.S. or $4.99 per book in Canada, plus 25¢ shipping and handling per book and applicable taxes, if any*. That's a savings of at least 15% off the cover price! I understand that accepting the 2 free books and gifts places me under no obligation to buy anything. I can always return a shipment and cancel at any time. Even if I never buy another book from Silhouette, the two free books and gifts are mine to keep forever.

235 SDN EEYU 335 SDN EEY6

Name	(PLEASE PRINT)	
Address		Apt. #
City	State/Prov.	Zip/Postal Code

Signature (if under 18, a parent or guardian must sign)

Mail to the Silhouette Reader Service:
IN U.S.A.: P.O. Box 1867, Buffalo, NY 14240-1867
IN CANADA: P.O. Box 609, Fort Erie, Ontario L2A 5X3

Not valid to current subscribers of Silhouette Special Edition books.

Want to try two free books from another line?
Call 1-800-873-8635 or visit www.morefreebooks.com.

* Terms and prices subject to change without notice. N.Y. residents add applicable sales tax. Canadian residents will be charged applicable provincial taxes and GST. Offer not valid in Quebec. This offer is limited to one order per household. All orders subject to approval. Credit or debit balances in a customer's account(s) may be offset by any other outstanding balance owed by or to the customer. Please allow 4 to 6 weeks for delivery. Offer available while quantities last.

Your Privacy: Silhouette is committed to protecting your privacy. Our Privacy Policy is available online at www.eHarlequin.com or upon request from the Reader Service. From time to time we make our lists of customers available to reputable third parties who may have a product or service of interest to you. If you would prefer we not share your name and address, please check here. ☐

SSE08R

LAURA WRIGHT

FRONT PAGE ENGAGEMENT

Media mogul and playboy Trent Tanford is being blackmailed *and* he's involved in a scandal. Needing to shed his image, Trent marries his girl-next-door neighbor, Carrie Gray, with some major cash tossed her way. Carrie accepts for her own reasons, but falls in love with Trent and wonders if he could feel the same way about her—even though their mock marriage was, after all, just a business deal.

**Available August
wherever books are sold.**

Always Powerful, Passionate and Provocative.

COMING NEXT MONTH